Hot Corner

Hot Corner:

Baseball Stories & Writing & Humor

by
Louis Phillips

Livingston Press

ISBN 0-942979-35-4, (HARDCOVER)
ISBN 0-942979-36-2, (PAPERBACK)

Library of Congress Cataloguing in Publication # 95-82134

Grateful acknowledgement is given to the following publications where these works first appeared: *Aethlon: The Journal of Sports Literature, The Christian Science Monitor, Elysian Fields Quarterly: The Baseball Review, The Nassau Review, National Lampoon, Saturday Review, Whiskey Island, and The Wisconsin Review, The Chicago Tribune,* and *Fan: A Baseball Magazine.*

Cover illustrations: David Gosselin
Illustrations, pages 136 and 138, Paul Whitson

Thanks to Melissa Boand, Beth Grant, Tamsie Pugh, and Tina Naremore for typing and proofreading. Thanks to Charles Loveless & Tricia Taylor for proofreading.

Typesetting and Book Design: Tina Naremore & Joe Taylor

Livingston Press
Station 22
University of West Alabama
Livingston, AL 35470

for

Lou, Lillian, Elizabeth, and Spencer Berger
good sports all

The author also gratefully acknowledges the following individuals without whose support much of this work would never have seen the light of day: Alfred F. Boe of San Diego University for his encouragement of all my baseball stories; Robert Kamon and Paul Doyle of the *Nassau Review,* my most faithful and steadfast home for my stories and poems; Steve Lehman, editor of *Elysian Fields Quarterly: The Baseball Review;* Mike Shenk, editor of FAN; Richard Gid Powers for his company at Yankee games; Bobby and Lyn Hoffman for making Little League Baseball an important part of the life of my family; and, of course, Joe Taylor, my good editor and publisher.

Table of Contents

Stories
&
Poems

The Day the Walrus Hit .400

Back in the 1930's and 40's, when the Charlotte Whips were top dog in the Carolina Triple A League, we had a player on our roster called "The Professor." Barrett Conley was his real name, but I never heard nobody ever call him that because a kid named Barrett has already got two strikes against him in life and that's what I think. We called him "The Professor" because he was the only one of the Whips who had ever seen the inside of a college and recognized it for what it was. I mean he was reading all the time, not comic books either, but real heavy stuff like novels, books that didn't even have no pictures in them. I tried stuff like that once or twice myself, but I don't see the sense in it, life being what it is. One picture is worth ten thousand words. That's what Abe Lincoln said. Or Ted Williams. One of those guys. And who's going to argue with them?

Anyway Conley hung up his spikes with a .294 lifetime batting average and with a trunk full of stolen bases, and so there he was looking around for something to do, because even with all that education he didn't know nothing about working, so he goes to Spike Kellings, who was the manager of that Cinderella team, the '41 Whips, and Spike suggests that The Professor handle the Public Relations side of things. The Professor thinks that over for a while and he says OK, and so Spike puts in a word with the management, and so that's how it happened that Conley became the Public Relations man for the 1946 Charlotte Whips. It made sense to us because Conley was always studying *How To Win Friends and Influence People.* He studied that book real good like some folks study the *Bible* because he always had a lot of friends hanging around him, asking him for tickets to the game or going out with him for drinks. He loaned the book to me once, but it didn't do me all that good, because I'm not really into reading, and I am really not into Public Relations. The way I look at it, people either like me or they don't, and if they don't, they can just lump it.

During the war years, the Charlotte Whips, like most sports teams, had a pretty rough time because there really weren't enough good players to go around. Anyone who could walk was called off to War, and the rest of us walking wounded had a difficult time getting hopped up about a ball game when we were thinking about old Adolf getting his. There were even a couple of years in there when the League had to close down all together, and if you don't think that made some of the owners hopping mad then you don't know a thing about owners. All the ones that I came in contact with would just as soon trade the silver out of your teeth as would look at you.

But, as I was saying, The Professor took on a pretty tough job. Getting people to come out to see Triple A ball is like pulling hen's teeth, and then you add on the fact that soldiers right after the war were staying home to save money and to work on their families, well then you can see right away that any PR man's got his work cut out for him. It would be just as easy to dig to China with a spoon.

So along about the middle of the '46 season, when the Whips were hovering around 3rd place, with the Mobile Oilers only a mere 2 and 1/2 games ahead of us, and our arch-rivals the Canton Tigers way out in front by 8, I mean 8 over the Oilers which means 10 and 1/2 over us, leaving us further back than the Little Red Caboose, we was only pulling in 500 to 600 fans a game, in a park that could hold a good 3,000, which is enough to break your heart, looking at them empty seats as if they were all beautiful and kind. After studying the situation day after day, and after roaming the empty stands like a mouse going through a maze, The Professor ups and ambles over to the box where the owner—Sonny Joe Terrel of the Bristol Distillery fortune—was sitting, with me sitting next to him because I had broken my arm falling out of a hammock, which didn't make the owner (I mean Sonny Joe and not the owner of the hammock, though she didn't feel none too good about it neither) all that happy with me. I was supposed to be playing second base part-time, but everybody knew I wasn't getting any younger, and I knew I was never going to make it up to the majors. Life can break your heart sometimes, and that, Sonny Joe would say, is more than your arm.

Anyway, after clearing his throat five or six times and staring down at his black and white shoes that had been specially shined for the occasion, since The Professor always believed in putting his best foot forward so to speak, he says to Sonny Joe, "Mr. Terrel, I got an idea about how to get you a lot of publicity."

"About time," Sonny Joe said, not taking his blue eyes off the game in progress. Sometimes he had a way about him that could make a grizzly vomit.

"I mean not just local stuff," Conley continued, "I mean real honest-to-God *Time* magazine stuff."

"*Time* magazine?"

"I'll throw in *Life* and *Look* and *Colliers*," added Conley, warming up to his subject.

Sonny Joe started chewing on the stub of his cigar like he was going to swallow the darn thing. *Time* and *Life*. Nothing could have warmed the cockles of Sonny Joe's heart more, that is if his heart had cockles. I once looked at some X-rays, and I never saw no cockles on nobody's heart, but then maybe I was holding the pictures upside-down. "So what are you standing here for?" Sonny Joe asked. "I'm paying you a good five grand a year to get me some attention, aren't I?" Out on the field, Hairpin Walsh, our utility infielder who was replacing me at second base, bobbled a hard-hit grounder. It done my soul good to see it.

The Professor gulped and swallowed hard. "But this could cost you a bit of money, sir. I mean you don't get something for nothing."

Sonny Joe looked up and placed his finger on the side of his nose, as if he were saying, son, are you telling me something I don't already know? "How much?"

When Sonny Joe asked *How much*, the whole world seemed to perk up. I mean Sonny Joe was used to spending gobs of money. Why, I myself seen him once give one of his very own ties to his star pitcher for Christmas. That's the kind of guy he was.

"I don't know precisely," The Professor said, "But I want to have enough so I can go up to Alaska and bring back a team of Eskimos."

"Go on," Sonny Joe said, removing his straw hat and wiping his forehead with his shirtsleeve. "You're going up to Alaska and bring back a team of Eskimos?"

"I mean there aren't any teams yet, but there will be when I get through. I'm going to get nine Eskimos together and teach them how to play baseball. Then we're going to stage a series of exhibition games all over the place, our team playing the world's first Eskimo baseball team, and that means packing them in. There won't be an empty seat in the place. And don't you think *Time* and *Newsweek* will come around to cover that?"

Sonny Joe didn't answer. He just leaned back into his seat and folded his arms across his chest like he was thinking, which I guess he was faking. Together we just watched Hairpin uncork a wild throw past the catcher, allowing the Mobile Oilers to score the winning run. I had a feeling that Hairpin wasn't going to be with our team much longer. Anyway, between us losing the game and The Professor's talk about Eskimos (he must have thought himself pretty clever bringing it up during a game when Sonny Joe couldn't give his full attention) there was a pretty thick pause flying in the air, a pause so thick that you could cut it with a butter knife. Finally, Sonny Joe pulled at his lucky green tie and turned his baby blues on me. "Is this guy crazy?" he asked.

"Who?"

"Him!" Sonny Joe chewed furiously on his cigar and jerked his thumb over his left shoulder.

"The Professor?" I had to admit that the question took me back. It had never occurred to me that Conley might not be playing with a full deck, but that sometimes happens with the college crowd. Some guy thinks and thinks and then his brains just sort of unwind like a cuckoo clock. I thought about the question for a while, and then said, "Nah."

"Thanks," Conley said, but he didn't look thankful. I guess he wasn't so happy that I took so long to answer.

I tried to make up for it by adding, "Maybe a team of Eskimos is just what we need. Of course I hope they don't bring their igloos with them, because they won't last long in this heat."

"Good," Sonny Joe said, tearing the cigar stub out of his mouth like it was a bad tooth. "You can help The Professor get the Eskimos in shape."

"Me?" I said.

"Yeah, you," Sonny Joe snapped. "You're no good to me with one bum arm."

I was going to say that I could play second base better with one arm than Hairpin could play it with two, but I held my tongue. My pappy used to say that you don't get ahead in this world by tearing other people down. Besides, Hairpin had enough troubles. It was pretty much an open secret that Sonny Joe was looking to trade him to the Canton Tigers, especially if he could pick up Truman "the ape" Hirsch, even if he was a catcher on his last legs.

Sonny Joe stood up and carefully buttoned his white shirt over his beer belly. "You might as well be earning your salary," he said. I didn't say anything to that either. After all, there is an old Yiddish proverb somewhere that says the man who pays your salary can give you a lot of lip. He slapped The Professor on his back. "Go get those Eskimos, Professor. I've always had a fondness for Eskimo Pies." He laughed; The Professor laughed; I just scrunched down in the blue wooden seat, thinking how some days it doesn't pay to be born.

And so that's why, one overcast day late in July, me and The Professor found ourselves standing in the Red Eye Saloon on the outskirts of Nushagak, Alaska. Actually, to be precise, Nushagak, Alaska, is all outskirts. It's outskirts from one end of town to the other. It was overcast, cold, damp, and I wasn't, to say it right out, happy. Enough's enough I thought, because I was one big ache from the top of my head to my big toe, and my butt was sore from sitting on trains for days on end, and then on the back of pick-up trucks, and then pushed sideways into a jeep. I mean I wasn't getting any younger, and if you're never going to make it into the Majors, there's no sense in pushing yourself over the edge. But over the edge was where I was. It just goes to show where a broken arm can lead you.

Anyway The Professor ups and ambles over to the bartender, who was about six-foot-four in his stocking feet, with a gold tooth, and a head that was completely shaved except for a thin stripe of black hair running down the center of his scalp. Everybody called him Whitey, which was funny because he was a black guy who looked as if he had eaten ground glass for breakfast.

The Professor asked him if he spoke Eskimo. "Hell, no," Whitey said. "Only Eskimos speak Eskimo. Do I look like an Eskimo to you?" All the old men along the bar, some six or seven of them, thought the remark was pretty funny and nearly fell down laughing. I didn't think it was all that funny, but then it was only ten in the morning and the place smelled as if it had been mopped down with bacon grease. The smell was pretty strong and it didn't do much for my sense of humor. "Why? Do you speak Eskimo?" Whitey asked.

"No," The Professor said, looking nervously back at me. "I'm looking for someone who can speak Eskimo. I'm willing to pay."

"How much?" Whitey shot back.

"Ten dollars a day, plus expenses." When I heard that I could have kicked myself for not speaking Eskimo. The trouble with being a baseball player is that your career is over too young, but if you can speak Eskimo, I bet that lasts you a whole lifetime.

Whitey poured a shot of straight whiskey into a dirty coffee cup and shoved it toward The Professor. "On the house," Whitey said, and Conley took it. He wasn't at all particular what he drank out of. The bartender held the bottle up for me, but I shook my head. After all, I was in training, and I didn't want to get unraveled too soon.

Whitey cocked his head to one side and scratched the back of his neck. "All right. I'll do it for you," he said.

But I thought you didn't speak Eskimo," The Professor answered, pushing the dirty cup forward for a refill. I changed my mind and decided to get drunk too. I was never one for making up my mind about things. Just add it to the list for all my reasons for failing.

Whitey grinned, his gold tooth shining. "I guess I forgot," he said. "But ten dollars a day, plus expenses jogged my memory. The Innuit will talk to me because I'm black. You watch. You just see how much easier I can make your lives."

I bet, I thought. Whitey took off his apron, folded it neatly, and laid it on the counter like it was a corpse. "Drinks are on the house, boys," he cried. The words were no sooner out of his lips when an avalanche of old duffers went spilling over the counter for all they were worth. Conley and I were out the door with Whitey right behind us. "I never did like the man I was working for," he said. I glanced back just long enough to see the patrons sliding over the floor, a whooping and a hollering like there was going to be no tomorrow. Of course how any of them could tell one day from the other in Nushagak is more than I could ever know.

"I wouldn't go back into that hell-hole for all the tea in China," Whitey said, adjusting the hood of his parka. I agreed. I wouldn't go back there either. But I had reasons of my own.

The Professor and me led Whitey back to the one-story building that served as our hotel, sat him down in something that passed for a lobby, and patiently explained to him what we wanted. Conley did most of the explaining because the project was his baby. I stared out the window a lot. There wasn't much to see, but whatever I saw there was a lot of it. Whitey got the gist of it pretty good, collected forty dollars in advance, money that I thought would be lost forever, and then he stood up and disappeared for a week.

Did you ever sit in a tiny hotel room in the middle of nowhere for a week? Let me tell you what it's like. There weren't no radio, so I didn't know what The Shadow was doing, though I had a pretty good idea how Yukon King was making out. There were no women, or if there was a woman she certainly wasn't my type. We couldn't even go back to the Red Eye Saloon, or what was left of it, because as The Professor pointed out, we were *persona non gratis* there, or whatever it was. I mean when the Saloon's owner came looking for Whitey, me and the Professor had to stand out on the roof to keep our heads from getting blowed off. We spent a lot of the week on the roof. We also spent a lot of the week playing Gin Rummy. The cards got worn so thin you could see your hand through the hands. Of course, I'm pretty good at Gin Rummy, and I don't mean to brag, but I must have won The Professor's monthly salary two times over, but there was nothing he could do about it. All he had with him to read was the Dale

Carnegie book and *The Immortal Poems of the English Language*. When he started reading the poems aloud, I chased him out into the street and nearly skinned him alive.

We were rolling back and forth in the street, and I had my knife out, and I was yelling into his ear, "If there's one thing a man don't want to hear about—it's a poem about nightingales. Maybe some college bum like you can stomach nightingales in North Carolina, but they don't stand up too well in the middle of nowhere. In the middle of nowhere a nightingale is about as useful to a man as a left-handed monkey wrench."

I nearly sliced The Professor's right ear off, but I didn't, and he forgave me because both of us were going stir-crazy. We went back inside and started to pack our bags, but who should show up but Whitey, followed by about a dozen Eskimo males. Following the males were about five females, with 18 or 20 children crawling all over them, and then some dogs and some sleds. I think there were five females. Everybody was so buttoned up that it was difficult to tell. The people had all their belongings tied to their sleds, and the children were bawling and carrying on something awful. Some of them had never been inside a hotel before. If we had been staying at the Hilton (fat chance of that!), we would have got ourselves thrown out. No doubt about that. I took one look at the group Whitey had brought back and I knew right off that Sonny Joe Terrel would blow a gasket once he got a load of all them mouths he had to feed. I kept my thoughts to myself, though, because I had almost cut Conley's ear off and it was his show anyway. I had to admit that the Eskimo women were beginning to look pretty good to me.

There were introductions all around, but most of the names just flowed over me like water off a duck's back. The leader seemed to be someone called Ootah. I nicknamed him The Walrus, and when our interpreter translated it, Ootah laughed and slapped his thighs. I took a liking to him right away. Then there was Attausu, whom I called Tuna, and then Seeglo, and somebody whose name sounded like Igloo. Anyway, you get the idea. The Professor had no better luck with names than I did, so he started calling them Nanook One, Nanook Two, Nanook Three, and so forth. It sounded like a pretty good idea, but the Eskimos turned out to be only human like the rest of us. They got hurt when we mangled their names, so I buckled down and tried to keep my mind to it for awhile. But it didn't do much good. Names are like anything else. If you're used to Sam and Fred and Joe and Choo-Choo, then a name like Egingwah is only going to knock around your tongue like a moose in a candy store. I remember The Professor showing me a Russian novel once, and everybody in there had three or four names, all of them a mile long. No wonder there is so much trouble in the world. Of course, my friend The Walrus really liked his nickname, but I knew right by looking at him he was the best of the bunch. It turned out that he was the only one of the bunch who really got the hang of hitting a baseball.

"Why do they call you Whitey?" I asked my interpreter.

"Because my name is Junior White," he said, not smiling. I guess his name was a sore spot with him too.

"What did you tell all these people?" Conley asked.

"Told them just what you said to tell them," Whitey said. "You're going to take them back to the States on a train, and when they get there, you're going to pay them to play baseball."

"Baseball," the Eskimos repeated in unison. It was the one word they all recognized. They repeated it solemnly. It became a chant. From their lips, from the mouths of people who had never even seen a baseball game, the word took on a holy quality. I felt I was standing in the presence of something special. I felt right at home with The Walrus and his friends, and to show my good spirit I took out an old outfielder's glove I had oiled and gave it to one of The Walrus's children to hold. Ooqueah didn't put it on, because he didn't know what it was for. He merely sniffed it, though I'm sure the oil wasn't what he expected. Then he took a big bite out of it. I didn't say nothing, though I was kinda curious about how it tasted.

"Tough, huh, kid," The Professor said. "How much did you say we were going to pay them?" he asked Whitey.

"Seal skins," Whitey said. "A lot of seal skins. Then you're going to put them back on the Great Iron Horse and ship 'em home. That's what you wanted me to tell them, isn't it, Boss?"

"Seal skins?" Conley asked. "We're not going to pay them in seal skins. You think we got a lot of seals in North Carolina?"

"They won't notice," Whitey said. Whitey had an answer for everything.

"What do you mean they won't notice?" Conley exploded. "They aren't deaf, dumb, and blind."

"They're going to be busy playing baseball right?"

"Right."

Whitey led me and The Professor off to one side. "All they really care about is the train ride. None of them have ever been on a train before. Just get them off the train, into the ball park, and back onto the train again. The seal skins will take care of themselves."

I bet, I thought.

"You owe me $200," Whitey said.

The color drained from The Professor's face. "$200? For what?"

Whitey grinned, flashing his gold tooth. "Ten dollars a day times three days, and the rest for expenses."

"Expenses? How can you spend $170 out here?"

"You want me to take the Eskimos back?"

"Give him the money," I suggested.

"I'll give you $30 plus fifty," The Professor said.

"You want to talk to my lawyer," Whitey suggested, narrowing his eyes.

"Sure, sure," Conley said, counting out five tens. "You got a lawyer?" The Eskimos were just standing around, holding their harpoons.

"I've got a lawyer, all right," Whitey said, and with that he took out his bowie knife and waved it under The Professor's nose.

"You got a good lawyer," I said.

Whitey nodded at me. "The best. He ain't never lost a case yet."

Conley sighed. He knew when he was beat, and he was being beat a lot lately. "All right, tell your lawyer to go back to his office, and I'll give you the full amount. But I want an expense account. My boss has got to have an accounting."

"I always give an accounting," Whitey said.

To emphasize his friendly feelings, Conley placed his hand on Whitey's shoulder. "Look, I'll give you a chance to earn even more money. You come back to the States with us, act as official interpreter, and I'll give you ten . . . make that twelve dollars a day, plus free room and board."

"In Charleston?"

"Charlotte."

"I'm not going South," Whitey said. "Why do you think I came all the way up here?" The pink palm of his hand was still up, so The Professor counted $200 into it. I kept thinking how much he owed me from the card games, and what I would spend it on. I always wanted a vacuum cleaner. I don't know why. Sometimes I get the craving for the strangest things. One year I bought eighty dollars worth of molasses just because it was on sale. "Up here, I'm treated well," Whitey said. "Me and the natives get along just fine."

"It's not what you think," Conley said. "Things are changing."

"What hotel is going to put us up? You thought of that?" he asked, folding the money and placing it inside a change purse that was hooked to the side of his knife belt. Both the purse and the belt were covered with tiny beads.

"Got it all figured out," The Professor said. "Look, you'll be working for us. The Charlotte Whips will look after you."

"You're going to look after me?" Whitey asked, scratching his top lip with the tip of his knife.

"Yep. And I'll give up fourteen dollars a day."

"I want twenty."

"Seventeen."

"Deal." Whitey and The Professor shook hands, and we all went back to the Eskimos. Whitey and The Walrus talked a bit.

"Neervoonga," The Walrus said.

"What did he say?" I asked.

"He wants to know when he's going to eat," Whitey said. "I promised them a good meal for coming this far."

"What else did you promise them? Diamonds?" I asked.

"Nobody's going to eat inside, until we figure out what we're going to do," Conley said.

The Walrus's kid had already eaten a good portion of my baseball mitt, and I was sick of blubber. Food was the last thing on my mind. I just wanted to get back home. Who would have thought that I would get homesick for Sonny Joe

Terrel?

"Tell them I'm only taking the men back to the States. We only want the men. The rest can go back home. I don't know why you brought the women and children," Conley snapped. I could tell he was growing a bit waspish from all the negotiations.

"They aren't going to go without their women," Whitey said. "Would you?"

"Never mind what I would do," The Professor said. "Just tell them what I told you to tell them." I could have told him that we ourselves came all this way without any women, but I didn't.

Whitey went back to The Walrus and talked a bit more. From my point of view there seemed to be quite a bit of back and forth confab. The dogs were yelping; the children were crying; and the men were waving their hands. Their harpoons didn't do much for my self-confidence. Whitey shook his head back and forth like he was watching a tennis match. "No, no," he said. "If they can't have their women, they're going home."

I shrugged. I couldn't blame them; but then, on the other hand, I couldn't blame Sonny Joe for not wanting to put out a lot of unnecessary money. Putting the blame on someone is tricky business; I guess it depends upon what side of the fence you're on.

I looked over to Conley and I could see panic in his eyes. In his heart of hearts he knew that Sonny Joe was going to go through the ceiling if we couldn't bring back what we had promised; on the other hand, Sonny Joe was going to go through the ceiling when he got a load of the bill for feeding and housing all them people. The best thing would be to go back and take the ceiling down right away.

"All right," The Professor said, holding up both hands like he was in a stick-up, which in a way he was. "You can all go. It just means that we can't go First Class."

When I heard that last sentence, I nearly swallowed my gum. Which reminds me. Did you ever try to chew gum in Nushagak? You have to be careful with it because it's tricky business, not just pop it into your mouth like you do back home. First, you have to warm it up some by laying it across the radiator—that is, when the radiator's working. Otherwise, if you walk outside with that stuff it breaks into thousands of tiny pieces. The chewing gum that is. Not the radiator. I've been meaning to tell Mr. Wrigley all about it sometime, but I ain't got to Chicago yet. As for the spiel about going First Class. There was no way on God's little green earth that we were going to go first class—ever. That's what it means to be in the Minor Leagues forever.

"But the dogs ain't going," said The Professor. "You got to figure out what to do with the dogs."

And so that led to another conference, with Whitey shuttling back and forth between us like one of those feathered things in a badminton game.

"The dogs are going," Whitey said.

"Look at the hair on those dogs," Conley screamed. "They'll die down there."

"You want to try to explain it to them, boss?" Whitey asked.

The Professor turned a deep blue. Some people might have figured it was from the cold, but I knew different. I could read The Professor like a book, and it wasn't one you could get out of the library, neither.

There was more back and forth, but Junior White knew where he had us, and so the upshot of all the arguing was that the Eskimos got their way. The farther you are away from home, the harder it is to strike a bargain that is going to favor you. So I got our stuff together and we all got on the sleds and the sleds took us to the train, and the train took us to another train, and soon we were going south. You could hear my sighs of relief all the way to Jacksonville.

As for the train ride to Charlotte, not counting the six hour lay-over in Flint, Michigan, I can sum it up in three little words, and the three little words that seem to sum up all of mankind's history—*It was a mess.* As far as I'm concerned you can count *a-mess* as one word. The Eskimos did just fine because they couldn't get enough of seeing all the new sights—and none of them understood ground that didn't have no white stuff on it—but The Professor and me were groggy from the brain down. Neither of us could see straight because, what with the dogs and all, we weren't getting much sleep. The dogs and the children were climbing over everything and exploring under everything, and all of them were moving so fast, that me and The Professor often got the children confused with the dogs. The conductor was always trying to put somebody off, and so Conley was always slipping somebody money, and while I was watching Conley paying off the conductor, someone or something bit me on the ankle. I don't know why, but it certainly was annoying not knowing who bit you. Maybe I was bit because Junior White—who, by the way, now insisted that he be called Mr. Junior, because he didn't want to be called, and who could blame him, Whitey in North Carolina—promised the new baseball team a land teeming with seals, and the best we were giving them was a long ride into free publicity. Did I say *free?* The word was enough to stick in one's craw. And to top off our troubles, the entire train smelled like fish. The Walrus and his gang had camped out in the aisles. The women had set up small kettles, and soon everything smelled like whales or seals or fish intestines. The Eskimos were generous and good-natured to a fault, but blubber didn't set well with me and Conley so we beat a quick retreat into the dining car, where we stared out at rushing-past scenery, and asked each other what the Foreign Legion might be like. We could have played Gin Rummy, but The Professor had already lost his shirt back in Nushagak, and Ooqueah had eaten the ten of clubs. Not that I was overly fond of the ten of clubs, you understand, but it does come in handy sometimes.

Then of course there was the weather. I mean here we were running into August, and the temperature was beginning to soar, and our friends didn't know what to make of it. They were pulling off their clothes left and right, and every time the train pulled into a station, me and The Walrus and Mr. Junior would hop off and go hot-footing for cakes of ice. I was pretty cool myself, but then I was brung up differently. What with all the Eskimos traipsing around half-naked—

I mean the women and everybody—well, we had to lock the doors on the coach and keep the blinds pulled down all the way. Of course, all kinds of rumors began to circulate, and soon there were local committees of all sorts—church groups, reformers, and even sinners—waiting for our train. I guess the groups were evenly divided, one half wanted to reform us, while the other half wanted to join the fun.

Some fun. I didn't feel no different than a swimming instructor on the Titanic. The dogs were going crazy, and two of them died before we hit upon the bright idea of shipping them back north in a refrigerated car. Eringwah went with them, which was too bad because he was one of the few of his tribe who was really beginning to understand the complexities and subtleties of baseball. Of course, The Professor had warned them about the dogs, so it took all our strength not to go around saying, "I told you so." We might have said, "I told you so," but we didn't know the words in Eskimo. As my sister used to say, the more you travel, the more you find out things you don't know.

Sending the dogs back with Eringwah was not the only bright idea I had. My mental stuff was working overtime, perhaps because there was so much brain food around. Fish is brain food, right? I don't know. I would have asked The Professor about it, but he was in no mood to talk about abstract ideas. He was worrying about Sonny Joe's pocketbook. Anyway, I knew we couldn't get the Eskimos off the train in Charlotte unless they had some clothes to wear, and so I thunk up the good idea of taking down all the measurements of the men, women, and children. I went around with my yellow tape and measured everybody. I think some of the women got a big kick out of it too, though I knew enough to keep my mouth shut and not let on how much I was enjoying my work. I telegraphed on ahead to a seamstress I know to get some clothes made up, and then The Professor and me decided to take a breather and get everybody off the train and into an empty field that bordered the tracks. It was there that me and The Professor and Mr. Junior really got down to schooling them in the finer points of hitting, running, throwing, fielding, and sliding. There's a lot more to the game than those few things, but you got to start somewhere.

The sun was out, but it was a good cool day, crisp, the kind you get every once in awhile during a Michigan summer. We got out a few bats and we started to zing the old apple around, and all of a sudden the world was different. I can't explain it exactly. You have to ask The Professor these things, not me. All I am saying is, it was different. We were throwing and hitting and laughing. Strike Attausuk. Strike Maggook. Strike Pingashoot. You're out.

Of course, it's only fair to point out that Mister Junior, who was six-foot-four, was the real star of the game. First of all, Ootah and Attausuk and Seeglo and all those guys took to Junior a lot more than they took to The Professor and me. He spoke their language and he looked more like them than we did, which is a shame because if it hadn't been for The Professor's idea, then none of us would have gotten together in the first place. And second, Mister Junior could really give the ball a good ride. The Eskimos were really good at finding things, or we would have lost the ball a couple of times. Mister Junior, in spite of his funny hair cut, could hit the ball as far as anybody I ever seen, and if he hadn't have been black, I could have touted him to the Whips. But there was nothing in life that I could do about that. Mister Junior knew it too, so on the way back to the train we didn't talk about it. My old man was like that too. If you don't talk about the bad things maybe they'll just go away.

What we talked about was the first time one of the Eskimos got a base hit. It was the top of the 1st and I was on the mound, just throwing easy, not trying to strike anybody out which I could have done pretty easy I guess, when Attasuk who I called Tuna, punched a little roller down the third baseline. Well, as soon as my team saw the ball go rolling, everybody went charging for it, and I just don't mean the third baseman either. The first baseman, the shortstop, the second baseman, the outfielders, the players on the other team, the women and children on the sidelines, everybody made a belly whop for the horsehide as if it were a mink with hiccups. I never seen nothing like it in my whole life. There was nothing but arms and legs and fannies hurling into the air, kicking up dust. It was like Times Square on New Year's Eve. Attasuk chugged up the line to first base. Good, I thought, somebody knows what to do. But when he saw how much fun all his friends were having, he cut across the diamond and jumped in. The Professor and me knew right away that this was an automatic out, but there are times in life when you enforce the rules and there are times you don't. Watching the pile of arms and legs got me to thinking that this was a non-enforcement time.

Finally, Seeglo with a stupid smile on his face came up with the ball and broke away from the pack. Attasuk saw Seeglo and started back toward first base. I was standing on the pitcher's—well, it wasn't exactly a mound at the time—spot, and Attasuk, who had enough fat on him to last out a couple of winters nearly bowled me over in the process.

"Let him go back to first," I shouted, but Seeglo missed the finer points of my logic. He uncorked the ball and caught Attasuk square in the back of his skull.

Seeglo leapt into the air. "Out," he cried, flashing a toothy grin and waving his arms over his head. "Out," he repeated.

Out in probably more ways than one I thought. Conley was fit to be tied. "This isn't dodge-ball," he told Seeglo. I don't know what Seeglo made of that. How could he know what dodge-ball was? As for Attasuk, he was lying face down in the dirt. Mister Junior was bending over him, shaking him. "You all right, Attasuk? You all right?"

Conley was pacing back and forth, pointing at people. "No throwing the baseball at anybody. Ever. You got that?" A couple of Eskimos nodded. "Especially no throwing at anybody's head."

Attasuk mumbled something to the ground. He reached back and patted the swelling on the back of his head, and then he went on mumbling. I looked at Mister Junior. "What's he saying?" I asked.

"He says baseball's too rough. He wants to go back to killing seals."

"He's not the only one," I said. There were times when I would get a craving to crawl away into an igloo myself. "Tell him it's not always this rough."

Conley was waving his team back into position, but nobody was moving. Everybody was watching Attasuk. Finally, Allakasignwah, who was Attasuk's ticklish wife, crossed herself and looked me straight in the eye. "Goode Okperegooptego kumageneakkategoot," she said to me.

I nodded and turned toward Mister Junior for a bit of help.

"She says that if we believe in God, He will take care of us."

"I hope she's right," I said.

Maybe it was her prayer. I don't know. But whatever it was, Attasuk revived, and me and The Professor and Mister Junior managed to restore order. Gradually the games resumed and gradually the magic crept back into the day. It frightened me how quickly The Walrus and his friends were picking up the game. I couldn't pick up dog-sledding as quick as they could pick up hitting a baseball.

After we survived the lay-over in Flint, and after me and Mister Junior arrived at a kind of understanding about our fates, Ootah tracked me down in the dining car. It was long after meal time, and I was just sitting at a table, half-heartedly picking at a kind of solitaire hitherto unknown to the world. Ootah sat down across from me. His eyes were kind of watery and I could tell that something was wrong, so I pretended to concentrate on my cards.

I turned over the nine of clubs which I knew right away wasn't going to do me any good, what with the 10 of clubs long gone. "No good," I heard Ootah say. "No good."

"What's no good?" I asked, without looking up.

"No good. Ootah."

I looked up then. Ootah was swinging an imaginary bat through the heavy air. "No hit, no hit, no hit."

"What are you talking about, Ootah? You hit the ball plenty good. You got nothing to complain about. By the time you play before the folks in Charlotte, you'll look like a pro."

"Pro?"

"Champion dog-sledder."

Ootah shook his head. He didn't believe me. "Attasuk," he said. "Maggook. Pingshoot. Out."

"You crazy, Walrus? You went four for ten."

"Kapsinik?"

I held up four fingers. "Four for ten." I pushed my fried egg sandwich toward him. It was cold and the yolk was running out of it, but, hell, it had to be better than Walrus toenails.

"Herrityennange," he said.

"Why not?"

"Four for ten." He held up his short stubby fingers. "No good."

"No good, no good. Don't you know any other English? Whoever taught you the words *no good* should get his head kicked in. Four for ten is the best. The best. Babe Ruth never went four for ten. Three for ten gets you into the Hall of Fame. Four for ten, not only do they put you into the Hall of Fame, they toss in the sun and the moon and stars as well."

Ootah remained stolid, his arms folded. He didn't believe me.

"You're a four hundred hitter and an eight hundred human being," I said. "Tukkesever?"

He understood, but he shook his head. "Four hundred hitter, good?" he asked.

"Four hundred hitter great," I said.

"Good."

"Great."

"Good."

"Great."

Ootah thought about that for awhile. He shook his head, then nodded up and down, smiling.

"Yes," I said.

"Good?"

"Yes."

He stood up, shook my hand, pumping it up and down like he was milking a productive cow. He waddled away as happy as a lark. Oh, hell, I thought. Maybe I oversold him. I was afraid that I oversold him and that he would become so in love with the game that he'd want to stay in Charlotte and play baseball forever. I knew that all The Professor and Sonny Joe wanted was a lot of attention, a couple of funny games, and then send them back to their igloos to melt in peace. I sat there, looking at the nine of clubs, feeling like a heel. I mean there are a lot of things you can say about life that are not true, but one thing you can say that is absolutely true, is that publicity is not everything. No, it ain't.

Ootah had gone four for ten, sure. But it was only a scrub game, and they were only scrub hits, off a pitcher who wasn't even trying to strike him out. In a couple of days, Rafferty Pinkhouse, one of the stars for the Whips, would step out onto the mound and make mincemeat out of him. And wouldn't the fans love it. And wouldn't Sonny Joe smile like he had swallowed a canary? Of course he would. I was so angry with myself for getting myself into such a mess that I took the cards from the table and chucked them from the window, watching the aces and diamonds scatter across the landscape. Don't think it wasn't a great loss neither, because that was my lucky deck. There were fourteen or fifteen of those cards that I could identify from the back if I were fifteen feet away, standing up to my ears in a coal bin.

The Professor had entered the car just in time to have seen me done it. He threw his hands up into the air and slid into the chair beside me. He removed a cigarette and tapped it on the tablecloth just like he always done. "What's eating you?" he asked.

"Nothing," I said.

"I thought those were your lucky cards." Conley searched for a match. "Gotta match?"

"How come you never got any matches of your own?"

"How come I don't have a million dollars?"

"Look, Conley," I said. "I'll give you a match if you send them home."

"Send who home?"

"Who do you think? Who have we been traveling with for the last four days until our underwear smells like it has been washed in tuna-fish oil, Tommy Dorsey and His Orchestra?"

Conley looked at me and shook his head sadly. "We're almost home and you're beginning to lose your marbles." He located a match so I didn't have anything left to bargain with. It wasn't much of a bargain anyway.

I was getting hot under the collar. "The Whips are only going to make mincemeat out of them. I know it. And you know it."

"The Whips ain't made mincemeat out of nothing all season long," Conley said. "So they'll have a little fun now."

"Some fun. What fun is there in it?"

"Fun? Who's talking about fun?"

"You. You were talking about fun."

Conley placed his huge hands behind his head and leaned backward on his chair like he was balancing on a tremendously thin wire. "I'm talking about making a living. That's what it boils down to, don't it? Everybody comes out ahead. The Eskimos get a free ride, get some grub, see some new land. Sonny Joe comes out ahead. You come out ahead. I come out ahead. The Whips come out ahead. The fans come out ahead. Everybody comes out ahead. What more out of life do we want than that? Everybody coming out ahead. That's what the game is all about."

"Somebody coming out ahead and somebody losing. That's what the game is all about," I corrected him.

"It doesn't matter if you win or lose. It's how you play the game," The Professor quoted. That was the trouble with trying to argue with him. As soon as you got him into deep water, he'd reach into his bag of tricks and drag out a poem or something and ride it like a raft to shore. All the time you'd be standing up to your eyeballs in rapids, the water spilling over your head like there was no tomorrow. "It's all that matters. Right?"

I couldn't think of an answer. I'm one of these people that always thinks of things too late. I should have a clause written into my contract that I could replay the previous year. I'm really good on the year that I've just been through.

"I'm going to let The Walrus play center field. What do you think? And they're all going to march onto the field carrying their harpoons. What do you think of that? If we don't make the cover of *Life,* I'm a monkey's uncle."

He was the monkey's uncle all right. I swung around in my chair and bopped him on the nose. It wasn't much of a punch because it's not easy to hit somebody when they're sitting in the chair next to you. If Jack Dempsey had to fight like that, he never would have been champ of the world. But it was the best I could do, thinking as I was, right off the top of my head. Besides, The Professor was in the middle of his balancing act when my love-tap landed, so he went over easier than an octopus milking a cow, hitting the table behind us and knocking it over into the next one. Table after table fell like it was a series of table-cloth covered dominoes. I can tell you that they don't make tables like they used to. Nor trains either.

I thought The Professor would bounce right back up and come at me with a series of haymakers, but the fall to the floor dazed him. It was a moving floor at that, and he just lay there, wiping blood from his nose with his shirt-sleeves.

"Help me up, you S.O.B.," he said. I guess he knew what I was sore about, but I didn't help him. He held up his arm and I didn't take it. He was still my friend, and we were still on the same team, but I just didn't feel like it. We went all the way to Charlotte and we never spoke a word to one another.

Of course the papers and magazines were full of it. They couldn't get enough of it, what with pictures of The Walrus and Sonny Joe and The Professor and Attasuk plastered all over the place. Everybody insisted it was the greatest publicity stunt in the history of the game, though a couple of sports-writers who were real blow-hards still favored the time that Spike Kellings tried to catch a softball tossed off the 30th floor of the Terminal tower in Cleveland. Spike had bet Sonny Joe $300 that he could catch a softball dropped from that height, and then at the last moment Sonny Joe substituted a grapefruit for the ball. The grapefruit was painted white and when it hit Kellings' huge catcher's mitt, the fruit split open and juice splattered all over him and into his eyes. Spike started screaming that he had gone blind, and everybody was doubled over with laughter. It was a good gag all right, and it got a lot of free publicity for the team. But it's the kind of gag that you can only pull once. More than once and it starts to lose its flavor. But how can a grapefruit compare to a team of Eskimos, that's what I want to know. I don't see no comparison at all.

Now I didn't want to go to that very first exhibition game between the Walruses and the Whips. I had made up my mind not to go, but curiosity finally got the best of me, plus I still wanted to keep on Sonny Joe's good side because he was the one still making it possible for me to pay the rent. Besides, in my absence, Hairpin Walsh had put together a hitting streak and had knocked nine home runs. Second base had never seemed so far away from me before. So there I was and Sonny Joe was strutting around like he had invented radishes or some other exotic fruit. Conley was in high spirits too. He was just going to sit back and let offers roll in from major league clubs that need a good Public Relations man. No way his career was going downhill.

Because the Walruses had come such a long way, the Whips let them be the home team. The first meeting was just going to be a one-inning contest before the regularly scheduled game with the Canton Tigers. After the first half-inning, the Whips had scored 13 runs against Ootah's team. The Whips would have scored a lot more, but some of the players, getting into the spirit of fun, started making deliberate outs and some of them tried some bonehead plays, such as stealing from second to first, when there was already someone on first. The fans were in high spirits too. They started tossing raw fish down to the field. I was getting hot under the collar, but there was nothing I could do.

Kirby "Pie-Boy" Armbruster was pitching for the Whips, and he could have struck out anybody on Ootah's team blindfolded, and so he started pitching underhanded, with everybody in the stands lapping that up. Finally Ootah came out and went to the plate and he struck out. He got so mad that he ran back to the dugout, got his harpoon, and he started chasing Pie-Boy all over the field. All the people in the stands thought it was a stunt, that it had been planned out, but I knew it hadn't been. Sonny Joe turned white in the face, and I knew what he was thinking—the Whips couldn't afford to lose any more pitchers. Sonny Joe started screaming things to the umpires, and finally Pie-Boy spilled down into the dugout, with the harpoon whizzing over his head. It struck the water-cooler and glass and water went spilling in all directions. Some of the Whips tackled Ootah, and the umpires mercifully called the game and cleared the field.

After the game, Ootah kept telling Conley, "Go home. We want to go home," but Conley was hearing none of that. Attasuk's wife had taken to praying for all she was worth. To soothe Ootah's ruffled spirits, Sonny Joe presented Ooqueah with a uniform all his own. I guess it made Ootah's son happy, but Ootah didn't smile. It was then I made up my mind what I had to do. I went back to the hotel, broke into Conley's room and stole a packet containing all the train tickets. I borrowed a pick-up truck from a friend of the woman who owned a hammock, waited until Ootah and his family and friends returned, and packed them all into the truck. Ootah was on my side. He was so disspirited that he offered no resistance, and besides the heat was nearly killing them all.

"Home," I told them. They didn't need to hear nothing else. I drove them all the way up the line to Danville, Virginia, knowing that we would be spotted at the Charlotte depot. I cashed in their tickets, bought them new ones, and put them on the first train north. And that was the last I saw of them. I would have gone with them myself, but there was nothing I could do in Nushagak. The thought of more fish and I would only break out into a rash. Besides I had to return my friend's truck.

On the way home, I passed by the ball park and stopped long enough to clear out my locker. After Sonny Joe heard what I had done, I wouldn't be playing for him. I'd be lucky to end up as a bat boy in Siberia. I got my gloves and took one last walk around. And who did I see sleeping under the bleachers but Mister Junior. He was sleeping off a drunk and I knew why. He hadn't been allowed to stay at the same hotel as Ootah and the others, and he wasn't allowed to play ball with them. I thought about waking him up and taking him home, but I didn't. There are times when it is better to leave well enough alone.

GREAT MOMENTS
IN THE HISTORY OF BASEBALL PROMOTIONS #1

Yankee Stadium declares
Catherine de Medici Day

All fans who come to the ballpark dressed as Catherine de Medici
receive a free baseball cap and an autographed copy of Ovid's
Metamorphoses

Momma Went and Bought a New Pair of Shoes

Momma went and bought a new pair of shoes. I knew what that meant. New shoes meant trouble. New shoes always meant trouble. Old shoes meant that you were comfortable in your old life. New shoes meant that a change was coming. The change was that Momma was planning to get married again, and if Momma's fourth marriage was going to be anything like the other three, then both of us were going to be spinning our wheels on a deep and muddy track.

It was 1953, and I was all of thirteen at the time, thirteen going on fourteen, and I was Momma's only daughter and so I was trying to be protective of her because I didn't want to see her crying no more. Momma would get on these crying jags and stay in bed for two or three weeks at a time. It could get pretty depressing, I can tell you that, and I had my own problems to take care of. Thirteen going on fourteen isn't the best age in the world. It's probably the worst age of all for a girl, especially a girl who has a mother who is not all that tightly wrapped, a mother who looks at marriage much the same way that Mae West looks at a grape.

Momma was a good-looker though, with lots of red hair, and a hourglass figure with the sand in the right places. She was nearing thirty-nine though, Jack Benny's age she said, and so I guess she was feeling loneliness was giving her the once over once too often, and she was spending a lot of money making long distance phone calls to old boyfriends and even an ex-husband or two. When those long distance blues get to you, it's time to sing another tune. So when Donnie "The Duck" MacGuire, journeyman third baseman for our one and only Charlotte Whips, turns up on our door-step, carrying flowers and candy and pitching the woo like the woo was a good old-fashioned spitball, well Momma starts losing her grip on reality and starts saying "Yes" all over the place. Next thing I know, Momma's got a new pair of shoes and I'm destined to be the step-daughter to a .249 lifetime batting average. It's nothing to do handstands over, I can tell you that.

Not that I have anything against Donnie "The Duck." Donnie's a fine young man. Yes-siree. He's blonde, thin as a rail, and a good twelve years younger than my old lady. I guess he's what everybody down home calls a nice guy. He doesn't know much, but he laughs a lot. That should give you something to think about. After all, what can a .249 hitter have to laugh about? Your career is on the line every time you come up to bat. I don't want to give the impression that Donnie "The Duck" is a moron, or anything like that. He's just good-natured, that's all. He'd give you the shirt off his back—but, of course, if you see the shirts he wears you won't be all that excited to get one. As I have said more than once, Donnie "The Duck" is good-natured, and Momma can wrap him around her little finger and still have room for Joe DiMaggio and Ted Williams and Stan Musial besides.

I could have wrapped Donnie "The Duck" around my little finger too, that is if I had wanted to, and so I had to be careful how I acted. I knew that if Donnie "The Duck" started giving me presents or started to show too much interest, Momma would have gotten awfully jealous, and that kind of trouble a daughter can live without. Not that Donnie "The Duck" ever bought me a great gift. An autographed photo of the entire Charlotte Whips, including the manager, the coaches, and the bat boy—all of them sitting down on the ground like a human watermelon patch—was never, in my book, going to compete with a diamond as big as the Ritz.

One day such thoughts reminded me to ask Momma why she wasn't sporting a diamond on the fourth finger of her left hand. The question didn't faze Momma. Some days it takes a stick of dynamite to get her going.

"Donnie's going to get me a diamond, Lulu," she said, not blinking an eye. Momma had a way of plucking her eyebrows that reminded me of a fingernail scratching down a blackboard. "Don't you pay the diamond situation no mind. Your momma's going to be sporting a diamond as big as anybody in this country's ever seen."

"I bet," I said, not really betting. A man who gives away autographed pictures of the Charlotte Whips is no big spender in my book.

"Mind your manners, Lulu," Momma said sharply, plucking at her left eyebrow. "A .249 hitter has more important things to worry about than buying a woman like me a diamond. I've had diamonds before. Now I want something more lasting. You deserve it. And I deserve it. A good-natured man makes up for a lot of diamonds."

I bet, I thought, but I didn't say a thing. I shut myself up like a pregnant oyster. And that's the way things stood until one Thursday afternoon, when I came home from Jefferson Davis High School and found Donnie "The Duck" sitting in our living room. He looked like he had been hit by a truck and the truck backed up just to make sure.

"Hiya, Donnie," I said, trying to act casual. I had just gone through cheerleading practice, and so I was pretty bushed myself.

Donnie didn't flash no goofy grin the way he usually did. He screwed up his face like he was fighting back tears. "Your momma tore up the wedding license," he said. That's all he said. "Your momma tore up our wedding license."

"Why did she do a stupid thing like that?" I asked.

"I guess she doesn't want to marry me," Donnie said. He sounded like he had struck out with the bases loaded. "It took us a while to get that license. We had to have blood tests and everything. Even went to the wrong window first. The man thought we were getting a hunting license."

I didn't want to hear no more of that. I stomped into the bedroom and found Momma sprawled out on the bed. She was fully dressed. Even had her purple hat on with the veil, and she was just wailing and wailing. I had a sudden longing to run back to school and stuff a dead chicken into somebody's locker.

"You tore up the wedding license?" I asked. It sounded like a good conversation opener to me.

Momma sat up and wiped her eyes. I found some wadded up tissue for her to blow her nose in. "We were just driving back from the License Bureau, and we started arguing about what kind of wedding to have, and I got so mad, I just took the license and tore the whole thing up."

"You were just making confetti earlier," I said. It didn't cheer her up none.

"It's only a wedding license," I said, but then I remembered that Momma was a lot older than me. I walked back into the living room where Donnie "The Duck" was practicing to be an undertaker. "She didn't mean to tear up the wedding license," I said. It didn't sound so good coming from me, but I figured someone had to say it.

Donnie's face lit up. "She didn't?"

"If I was you," I told him, "I'd march right in there and patch things up. You can always buy another license."

"It's two dollars," Donnie said. I shrugged my shoulders and went into the kitchen to make myself a peanut-butter and jelly sandwich. Then I poured out a big glass of milk. I did it all in a very casual manner. My friends at school would have been very proud of me. Donnie went into Momma's room, and there was a lot of talking back and forth, and when they finally came out, with Donnie's arm around Momma's shoulder, I could see that everything was all right. I guess I had figured that Momma's getting married wouldn't do me no harm, especially with Donnie bringing home a lot of his baseball-playing friends.

Momma tugged at her skirt. "You run over to Grandma's and wait for us there," she said.

"What for?" I asked in my super-casual manner.

"Because young lady, Donnie and I have to go down to the License Bureau and get another license, and I don't want you to stay here by yourself."

"This time we are going to get a license written on steel so your Momma can't tear it," Donnie "The Duck" said. He let loose a guffaw and then they were out the door, Tweedledum and Tweedledee. Poor Momma, I thought.

I walked over to Grandma Walsh's and along about six-thirty, quarter-to-seven, Donnie's moth-eaten station wagon pulls up and out step the two lovebirds as if nothing at all had happened. Momma tugged at her skirt, and Donnie punched his hat around before putting it back on top of his head. His hair was so thin and fine that at a distance he looked bald.

Grandma Walsh, who was 83 at the time, with skin like leather and a tongue to match, was fit to be tied. Her own daughter hadn't told her about getting married again, and that wasn't the worst of it. The worst of it, from Momma's point of view, was that Grandma wasn't all that fond of Donnie "The Duck." She always called him "That Fool!" It's little things like that that put a damper on family relations.

"Well, you went and done it this time, Miriam, didn't you?" Grandma said, leaning forward in her rocker, her arms folded tight across her stomach like she had a bellyache. When Donnie climbed up the steps, Grandma started moving that rocker like it was a tank. She stuck out her tongue, but Donnie had been through it all before. He took it in stride. "Good afternoon," he said, tipping his hat. He tossed me a wink, which was his way of saying that I had done good work a few hours before, getting him and Momma back together again.

"It's not afternoon. It's evening," Grandma said.

"You're right about that, Mrs. Walsh." Donnie "The Duck" sunk into the second rocker and pounded his right fist into his left palm. "I feel so good thought I'd take you all out to eat this evening." Two months before, Donnie had called Momma's momma "Grannie." We never did hear the end of that one.

"Why don't you get a job like a normal person?" Grandma asked. She had gotten Donnie into her sights and she wasn't going to let up.

"Oh Momma," Momma wailed.

"Why don't you come down to the park and see me play sometime?" Donnie asked, grinning from ear to ear.

Grandma raised her head and sniffed the air. "I'd rather go to a funeral home and watch the bodies rot."

That remark broke Donnie "The Duck" all to pieces, and he was almost falling out of his chair.

"Fool," Grandma spat.

What Donnie "The Duck" didn't understand about Grandma was (and I know it doesn't make any sense to say it, but it is God's own truth) that she didn't really like people to laugh at her jokes. Grandma would say the weirdest things sometimes, but if you laughed, she would look at you as if you had thrown up in church.

Momma paced back and forth on the porch, clutching the brand new marriage license for all it was worth. I could tell that Momma was worried. She was biting her lower lip and looking daggers at Donnie.

"You two hitched or not, Miriam?" Grandma asked. I always like to listen to my momma getting chewed out by her own momma. It did my heart good.

"We just got the license this afternoon, Momma," my momma said. "We ain't had time to get married yet."

Donnie came up for air. "Hey, Miriam, did you hear what your momma said about going down to the funeral home and watching the bodies rot?" he asked. For an answer, Momma kicked him in the shins.

Donnie clutched his leg. "Auugh. What was that for?"

"Nothing," Momma said. "Nothing at all."

Grandma held out her boney hand. The back of it was all covered with brown spots—liver spots was what Grandma called them. "Can I see your license, Miriam?"

Momma raised one plucked eyebrow. "What for, Momma? It's just like any other marriage license."

"I know, child, but I ain't seen one in a good long while."

Momma sighed and gave the piece of paper to me. I passed it on to Grandma. Donnie followed this slow progress like we were moving gold. Grandma took the license and pretended to read it. Donnie rocked back and forth, smirking. "Well, Mrs. Walsh, maybe you and I should try and bury the hatchet," he said.

But Grandma just sat there, rocking, tearing the license up, tearing it into a thousand pieces. "Momma!" my momma cried, but she was too late. Donnie's jaw dropped all the way to his knees. He couldn't believe he was seeing what he was seeing. Momma was down on her knees, trying to gather up the pieces. Tears streamed down her face. Even if she hadn't been my momma, I would have felt sorry for her. I tried to help Momma, but we were only getting in each other's way. Donnie didn't move. He didn't do nothing. He didn't say nothing. He just sat there as if he had swallowed a horse.

"Oh God," Donnie groaned.

"Don't you curse on my front porch," Grandma said.

"Momma? Why did you tear up my marriage license?" my momma asked.

Grandma just kept at her rocking, working at it like it was her only profession. "I don't know what came over me, Miriam. I just couldn't help myself. That's how it is when you get old. Things come over you and you just can't help yourself."

"Oh God," Donnie groaned again.

"I told you before, Mr. Big-League baseball player. I won't have no more cursing on my front porch." Grandma tugged at her gray sweater and reached for her cane.

Momma backed off, thinking that any minute Grandma might start swinging. With her cane, Grandma was a good .300 hitter. "Besides, child, it's no big thing to bother your head about. You can always get another license."

"Another one?" Donnie asked, raising his head out of his hands. "Another one? I already got two."

"See Miriam? He says he got two. Who else is he planning to marry?"

Momma stooped picking up the pieces. Sometimes the pieces of things don't do anybody any good.

As you might have guessed, the next morning found the three of us—Donnie, me, and Momma,—bright and early at the Marriage License Bureau, a dark cubbyhole of an office set on the third floor of City Hall. Mrs. W. Dunnigan, a pouty-faced woman who wore her hair in a bun and resembled a pigeon, didn't looked too thrilled about seeing Donnie again. I knew it was Mrs. W. Dunnigan because that's what the little wooden block on her counter said.

Mrs. Dunnigan stood behind a little half-door-like affair and tapped her pencil against the counter top. "I think I have seen you two before. Haven't I?"

Donnie "The Duck" studied the tops of his shoes. They were pretty beat up and in need of a good polishing. I guess he was waiting for his wedding day before getting them shined—that is, if there ever was going to be a wedding day. I studied the electric fan over my head. For some reason, Mrs. Dunnigan reminded me of two-week-old milk.

Momma jabbed Donnie in the shoulder. She wasn't in a good mood because she hadn't gotten much sleep the night before. "The woman's talking to you, Donnie."

Donnie nodded. He knew the woman was talking to him. To him and no-body else. He cleared his throat. "Well Ma'am. You see, we had a little accident."

"Speak up. I can't hear you," Mrs. Dunnigan said.

"The woman can't hear what you're saying," Momma told Donnie. I kept looking at the fan and wishing I was dead. Standing right behind us were two teenagers. They looked as if they were in an awful hurry to get married. From what I had seen of marriage, I couldn't understand why anyone would want to go to the bother.

"We had a little accident," Donnie said.

"Accident? What do you mean by accident?" Mrs. Dunnigan demanded.

"That's what I'm trying to tell you, Ma'am," Donnie said, his eyes not lift-ing from the tops of his shoes.

"You don't have to sass me, young man."

"For God sakes, Donnie, tell her," Momma said.

Mrs. Dunnigan folded her hands and placed them out in front of her as if she was praying. "I have better things to do than to issue you the same marriage license over and over again."

"I know Ma'am. I really do."

"Do you?"

"I really do."

"Ma'am," the pimply-faced boy behind me said.

Mrs. Dunnigan waved him away. "Be with you in a minute. Marriage lasts a lifetime. It can wait a few minutes."

"My dog chewed it up."

"What?"

"The marriage license? My dog chewed it up."

"That's what I thought you said."

"So if you could just issue us another license, we'll be on our way. We won't bother you no more."

Donnie "The Duck" looked so pathetic that I guess he touched a soft spot in Mrs. Dunnigan's pouty little heart. "All right. For another two dollars, I'll issue you another license. But this had better be the last one."

"Yes, Ma'am."

"But you'll have to wait because I'm going to take care of these young'uns first." She waved the pimply-faced boy and his pregnant girlfriend to the head of the line. I went out into the hallway to find the water cooler. After about thirty minutes, Donnie and Momma came out, and we went to Donnie's car.

"Why don't we get married today before we lose this thing," Donnie sug-gested. It was the first smart thing I had heard him say in a long time.

"Because I want my momma to be there when I get married, that's why," my momma said. She opened the glove compartment in Donnie's car and tucked the marriage license in there for safe-keeping, sliding it under a map of North Carolina. "Besides, you have got a game this afternoon with the Canton Tigers. Or have you forgotten that?"

"No, Miriam, I haven't forgotten," Donnie said, driving away like he had just robbed a bank. "But your momma's not going to come to our wedding. She doesn't like me."

"She'll come," Momma said. "Momma always says she won't come, but she always comes. It's kind of a good luck charm." There was a lot I could have said about that, but I didn't. Donnie took us home and went off to the game. Even I knew that .249 hitters don't forget when they have games to play.

I was in the middle of the Civil War when the phone rang. Momma talked for a few minutes, and she started to cry and started to curse up a storm, which really wasn't like Momma at all. Then she hung up. Then she sat down and started to laugh. Soon the laughing and the crying were all mixed in together. Finally she said, "Donnie's had his car stolen."

"Stolen?" I wasn't thinking about the car.

"He came out to the parking lot after the game, and the car wasn't there." Momma wasn't thinking about the car either.

"Maybe one of his friends borrowed it," I suggested. All of a sudden I understood what my teacher had said about the start of the Civil War. I don't know why I understood it, I just did.

"He's reported it as stolen." Momma's eyes were beginning to get puffy.

"Nobody would want that old heap," I said. "If people were going to steal cars, why don't they steal Cadillacs and leave the old ones alone?"

"I shouldn't have put the license in the glove compartment," Momma said.

I agreed, but couldn't say I agreed. In our minds, it had become "The License." I pretended that I was studying my history lesson, but it was no use. "Who won the game?" I asked as casually as I could.

"I didn't ask," Momma said. "I didn't ask."

Momma didn't relish going back down to City Hall and trying to get a license, "The License," from Mrs. Dunnigan, and nobody could blame her, but Donnie "The Duck" wasn't going to go in there alone, nobody could blame him either. It wasn't his fault that the car was stolen. If he said that once, he said it a thousand times. Donnie asked if I would go with him, and I reluctantly said yes. I figured it was in Momma's best interest, and so I went.

"What now?" Mrs. Dunnigan screamed when she saw Donnie and me coming through the door. The stack of files she was carrying fell to her feet. "You want to marry her, too, I suppose," she said with a great chill. She meant me.

"I don't want to marry her," Donnie said. He meant me. "I want to marry her mother." Before coming into the office, I had given Donnie a little pep-talk, warning him to be more assertive.

"So go marry her," Mrs. Dunnigan said. "that's across the hall, not here."

Panic set in. "But I need another license," Donnie blurted out. "My car was stolen."

Mrs. Dunnigan took three steps back as if someone had punched her. "Your what?"

"His car was stolen," I said.

Mrs. Dunnigan breathed a sigh of relief. "Oh, so you're talking about a driver's license this time."

"No, ma'am, a marriage license."

Mrs. Dunnigan raised an eyebrow. "Another one?"

"It was in the glove compartment of the car," I said.

"And the car was stolen," Donnie added.

"But I've given you three licenses already," Mrs. Dunnigan said. Even I could sense the despair in her voice. She wasn't casual about it at all.

"My car was stolen," Donnie repeated. "It wasn't my fault."

"You shouldn't have kept it in the car," she said. "It was the third one I gave you. Your shouldn't have kept it in the car."

"I couldn't agree with you more, ma'am," Donnie said. "But I didn't know that my car would be stolen."

Mrs. Dunnigan frowned. Donnie "The Duck" took out a twenty-dollar bill and held it limply in his hand. He wasn't quite sure what to do with it. I took Donnie's elbow and pushed his arm forward.

"What's all this about?" Mrs. Dunnigan asked.

"For another license, ma'am," Donnie said.

Mrs. Dunnigan drew herself back. "Are you trying to bribe a city official?" she asked with great indignation.

Donnie drew his arm back. "Oh, no ma'am."

Mrs. Dunnigan didn't pick up the folders she had dropped. She stepped over them and walked behind her counter. She adjusted her name plate. "I'll tell you what," she said at last. "This is it. You lose this one, I suggest you move to another county. I don't want you to come back in here again. You understand?"

"Yes, ma'am," Donnie said, shifting his weight from one foot to the other.

"It's no joke, ma'am. I didn't think my car would be stolen." He was so sincere, no one could doubt him. Mrs. Dunnigan took out an old pen and began to write.

"Maybe you could give me two, just in case?"

Mrs. Dunnigan glanced up from her writing. From the expression in her eyes, no reply was needed.

"Yeah. Well, one would be plenty," Donnie agreed. I studied the fan over my head. It hadn't changed a bit since our last visit.

Outside the building, Donnie offered me the license, but there was no way on God's earth I was going to be responsible for it. I would have preferred to take a job guarding Fort Knox.

"Just take it to your momma," Donnie "The Duck" pleaded.

"You take it to her," I said.

"But I've got to go to the ballpark."

"I don't care. I'm not taking it," I said. He stood with me until the bus came.

I got on it and waved good-bye. As I said, I was fond of Donnie. And if he made Momma happy, so much the better for me.

That afternoon the Charlotte Whips trounced the Canton Tigers 12 to 3. The players were all in a high mood and some of them went down to "Davey Jones's Locker" for a few beers. About six hours later, I heard this tapping on my bedroom window. I was up late studying for my history test, and when I heard the tapping, I got scared. But it was only Donnie "The Duck."

"What are you doing?" I asked him, opening the window slightly. I was afraid that maybe he was going to start something with me, that maybe the woman from the License Bureau had put ideas into his head. Anyway, it was easy to see that Donnie had been drinking. A lot.

"I've come to say good-bye," Donnie said.

"What do you mean good-bye? Are you and Momma going somewhere?"

"I don't have no license," Donnie said.

"What do you mean you don't have no license? You and I just got a new one this morning."

"I lost it in the bar."

"Well, go back to the bar and get it. I won't tell Momma. Just go get it." I was beginning to feel sick to my stomach.

I can't," Donnie moaned.

"Why not?"

"John 'The Moose' Berger tossed it down the toilet."

"Tossed it down the toilet?"

"We were just having a little fun, and when I told them about my marriage license being stolen, they started fooling around, and 'The Moose' grabbed it out of my hands and ran to the men's room and flushed it down the toilet. He thought it was pretty funny. I didn't think it was funny."

"What are you going to do?" I asked.

"I don't know," he said. He looked so sad, so defeated, I felt I should have taken him in my arms and cradled him on my breasts. But I didn't. I slammed the window down and turned off the lights. I cried myself to sleep.

Two days later, Momma bought herself a new pair of shoes. Blue satin pumps. They were quite handsome and very expensive. We no longer talk about her marrying Donnie "The Duck." But at least the new shoes made her feel better.

Johnny Inkslinger Returns To Mudville To Cover An Exhibition Game Played By Ghosts

It is so austere—this town without baseball,
5,000 fans or so departed to other lives,
Anubis digging in at home plate,
Parched outfield barely breathing under leaves,
So much hope in a deserted stadium,
The scoreboard muted 4 to 2.
Cooney walked this infield, & Barrows.
So did Flynn who was a hoodoo—
So despised. Was he a true fake?
The sky beyond the fence is emblazed
With the Constellation Slow Curve
That has lead so many to an early death.
A portable radio in the dugout plays:
George "Fathead" Thomas on sax,
"When Did You Leave Heaven?"
Ah! No heaven without baseball,
Without a muffin-headed skipper
Signaling the suicide squeeze,
The margravial Umpire up to his hips
In pop bottles—**STRIKE THREE!**
Urchins scampering from their miggles
To shout like mustard in bleachers,
The prodigal infield rehearsing
The unassisted Triple Play,
The Relief Pitcher parading
His nervous stomach like a banner.
Even in another Galaxy, there is a Casey,
A smile of Christian Charity upon his lips,
The winning run dancing in his head.
Jazz & baseball:
They are American to a fare-thee-well.
Bad cess to any fool who contends
That Baseball is only a game.
Batter up!

Why Paul Bunyan Is Not
in Baseball's Hall of Fame

Every dyed in-the-wool baseball fan in America, and maybe even in Japan for all I know, has probably wondered what would happen if the great Paul Bunyan had ever took it in his head to play baseball. There's no doubt, most people think, that Paul could have out-pitched Charles Hoss Radbourn and Wild Bill Donovan and still have hit a couple of thousand home runs at the same time. A place in Baseball's Hall of Fame at Cooperstown would have been his for the asking.

In point of fact, however, (though his name is not to be mentioned in the annals of the game: *The Encyclopedia of Baseball* makes no mention of him) Paul Bunyan did try his hand at major league baseball. Unfortunately, not everything in life works out the way it's supposed to. Paul's performance in the big leagues is just one more example of the truth of that saying.

Now we're talking quite a few years back, you understand. One fine morning when there was still a bit of chill in the morning air, America's greatest logger sat down to a heaping platter of griddle cakes, sausages, and coffee. I tell you the platter of griddle cakes was stacked so high that the top griddle cake was pressed right against the ceiling of the Old Home Camp Mess Hall. That's why Hot Biscuit Slim, the camp's cook, always brushed the ceiling over Paul's table with syrup and melted butter. As for the coffee, it was poured into a cup so large that it would take the strength of two ordinary men just to lift it off the table. Why one morning, Babe—Paul's giant ox—accidently hit the cup of coffee with her tail and the brown liquid went running out with such force that it became a river. I think today people call it the "Big Muddy" or the Mississippi (which is one reason why it's so brown—the grounds from Paul's coffee haven't yet settled). Now you don't have to believe me. There were others who were there who saw the whole thing. Three Day Johnny Long would have drowned in the brew if Paul hadn't grabbed him by his hair and yanked him out. Three Day was pretty grateful to Paul after that, for nobody wants to be remembered for having drowned in a cup of coffee.

As I was saying, Paul sat down to breakfast and opened his newspaper— THE MONUMENTAL LOGGER'S LEDGER AND EVENING SUN TIMES NEWS—and opened to the sports section. After studying the sports column and seeing how much attention little bitty common men were getting for hitting a little ball, Bunyan looked up, scratched his head, and rubbed his chin. Whenever Paul did that, you knew he was thinking, thinking up a storm.

"Look-ee here, Babe," he said to his bright blue ox, "I have been logging most of my life, and I'm beginning to think that maybe it's time for a change. I think I'm going to take this summer off. I'm going down to Minneapolis and become a ball player."

Paul turned around on his bench and faced Johnny Inkslinger. "Johnny," he said. "I want you to do me a favor. I want you to write all the baseball clubs and see if any of them can use me to play for them. After all, if I'm going to give up for a summer, we're going to have to get some money back."

"Sure thing, Paul," Johnny said, and he took out his pen, took out a stack of paper, and soon he was turning out letters as fast as Paul could chew down griddle cakes. Naturally all of Paul's loyal crew—Johnny Inkslinger, Hot Biscuit Slim, Three Day Johnny Long, Snoose MacGinnis, etc.—were sad to hear Paul was giving up logging, but they understood what a great temptation lay before him. Who could deny Paul Bunyan the opportunity to become the greatest baseball player of all time?

And so while Johnny Inkslinger (who was the only man on Paul's crew who could write) was sending out letters, Paul took up his great axe and he and Babe trudged off to the woods. "I gotta make me a bat," Paul said, "and it can't be no ordinary bat. It has got to be a bat to allow me to do superhuman feats. The history of the game of baseball has to be in the wood, and the wood has to be as hard as iron. Won't do me no good to go down there with bats that break in my hands."

For miles around, for days on end, for nights on their side, men, women, children, and sundry small animals as far away as Jack Fish Lake, Saskatchewan, could hear Paul's axe whistling in the wind, and it wasn't whistling *Dixie* either. Down came a good dozen trees before a poor body could utter Jack Robinson— and these were good-sized trees too, not the tiny toothpick splinter trees you see nowadays on the sidewalks of cities. When I say trees, we're talking trees. Oak. Ash. Pine. *Boom, Boom, Boom* roared Paul's mighty axe, and then out he whisked his pocket knife, and while Babe, the blue ox, looked on, Paul whittled himself two dozen of the finest baseball bats ever to see the light of day.

One by one, Paul took up his bats and tested them. The years of tree-felling had honed his swing into perfection. Why, to see Paul Bunyan swing a bat was to see pure beauty; to hear Paul Bunyan swing a bat was to hear the wind blowing across the ocean.

"Now I just need some baseballs to hit," Paul announced to himself and Babe. But there were no baseballs to be had. Finally someone—I think it was Saginaw LeGrec—remembered the biscuits made by Uncle Boss. Those biscuits were as round as any baseball and just as hard, so LeGrec rounded up a couple of dozen biscuits, and he and Johnny Inkslinger took turns pitching. Johnny had a pretty good curve ball, and Saginaw had a fast ball that some reporter had clocked at 100 miles per hour, but no matter how hard or how sneaky those two loggers threw, Paul couldn't miss. *Boom! Boom! Boom!* With a mighty swing of the bat, Paul sent Uncle Boss's biscuits all over creation. That's why even today people in the Sahara desert might stumble upon a stray biscuit and not know how it got there. It got there because Paul was swinging for the fences. I bet even a few biscuits landed on the moon, but I don't want to be accused of exaggerating.

Now while Paul was axing, whittling, and taking batting practice against Johnny Inkslinger and Saginaw LeGrec, Old Home Camp was being turned into a northern outpost for major league scouts. As soon as word got out that Paul had taken it into his mind to play major league baseball, the telegraph wires were humming, the phones were ringing, and the baseball contract writers were working overtime. Everybody wanted Paul Bunyan to play for their team, and poor Paul's brain was starting to burst.

"I never saw a mortal hit a baseball like Paul Bunyan," the scout for the New York Yankees said. "Not even Babe Ruth himself. Imagine a line-up of Ruth, Pipp, and Bunyan. Why nobody would ever beat us again."

"Offer him whatever he wants," the owner of the Yankees wired, but his instructions didn't differ from the instructions of any other baseball team owner. The image of Paul Bunyan hitting home runs caused more excitement than a flock of fleas at a dog-judging contest.

Day and night, agents, fans, owners, and lawyers did everything in their power to get Paul to sign on the dotted line, but Paul refused to be rushed. He wanted to do what was right. At first he suggested that, just to be fair, he could play one week with every major league club, but the Commissioner of Baseball refused to allow such a thing. It would create a dangerous precedent. If Paul could play one week with one club and then a second week with another, soon every player might ask to do the same thing. If such a thing happened, the baseball pennant races would be in shambles. Utter shambles.

Finally, Paul, after talking things over with Johnny Inkslinger and Hot Biscuit Slim, decided there was only one way to play baseball. He would put all the names of major league teams into a hat and Paul would draw one name out. Paul would sign with whatever team he drew by lot.

On the day of the big drawing, Johnny Inkslinger painstakingly printed out the names of all eighteen major league teams (there were not the twenty-four teams that we have today) and dropped them into a hat borrowed from a scout from the Boston Braves (not the Atlanta Braves we know today). The mess hall of Old Home Camp was packed with wall-to-wall reporters, scouts, agents, managers, and just plain baseball fans. Paul was blindfolded and then he put his hand into the cap and pulled out a slip of paper. Johnny Inkslinger took the paper and opened it. He paused. The suspense was thicker than one of Hot Biscuit Slim's flapjacks. "Paul has drawn the Cleveland Indians." The name of the team had no sooner left Johnny Inkslinger's lips when a great commotion burst out in the dining hall. Reporters, dashing for the nearest telegraph office, knocked over chairs and each other. Some scouts and managers not associated with the Cleveland team fainted dead away. The members of the Cleveland Indians who were present at the drawing were jumping up and down, and hugging and pounding each other for joy. The owner of the Boston Red Sox, however, moaned so loudly that some of the inhabitants of Canada had thought that Paul's blue ox had died, or at the very least, was suffering from a terrible stomachache.

As for Paul, he studied the piece of paper, and his heart fell to his boots. In truth he had been hoping to play for the New York Yankees, but because he was a man of his word, he smiled and abided by the decision. "It's the luck of the draw," Johnny said. He had known Paul a long time, and he could sense Paul's disappointment.

Tris Speaker, who was a great center fielder for the Indians, and perhaps the greatest center fielder of them all, jumped up from his chair and grabbed Paul's hand. "I'm mighty glad that you're going to be on our team," Speaker said. Seeing the Gray Eagle (a nickname given to Speaker) made Paul feel a lot better about his new team. Paul, in fact, began praising Gray Eagle to the skies. He praised Tris Speaker so highly that the Gray Eagle began to blush bright red. Finally, Speaker stammered, "Now, you, you, you get dressed, Paul, and I mean . . . packed . . . and I'll drive you down to the train station myself. With any bit of luck, we'll be able to get you into the series against the Senators."

And so the great Paul Bunyan packed his bats, made final arrangements for the care and feeding of his big blue ox, Babe, he shook hands with his fellow loggers, and off he went to Cleveland, with visions of glory dancing in his head. All across the nation, the newspapers and radios blared out the news:

Paul Bunyan Goes To Cleveland;
Is The Pennant Race Over?

But Paul Bunyan, unfortunately, wasn't able to play against the Washington Senators. He had to sit in the stands and watch. Why? Because nobody had a uniform big enough for the new star. "The first problem," the owner of the Indians told the sports reporters, "that we have to solve is to find a uniform that Paul can wear. After all, Paul can't tear down bases in those boots of his."

When Paul heard that he just roared with laughter and the reporters joined in. There never before had been so much laughter in Cleveland.

You may not believe me, but I'm only telling the truth when I say that it took two weeks and over thirty tailors working around the clock to make Paul Bunyan's uniform. It took forty or fifty shoemakers, working morning, noon, and night to make Paul's shoes. The spikes on those shoes had to be just right. Another fifty men and women worked around the clock stitching Paul's outfielder's mitt, for it had been decided that Paul would play in the outfield. It didn't seem likely that any player could ever hit a ball over Paul's head. Tris Speaker, who was some say the greatest center fielder ever to set shoes upon grass, graciously decided to move over to right and allow Paul to take center stage. "The game comes first," Speaker said. "What's good for the game, is good for me, is good for the team, is good for us all." The Gray Eagle was not short of good sportsmanship.

By the time Paul's uniform and shoes and mitt were ready, it was already the closing days of July, and the Indians were on their way to Boston to play an exhibition game with the Braves. (Cleveland had a three-game series with the Red Sox later that week.) Ehmke was to pitch that day against the Indians, so it was decided that Speaker would start, and that Paul, since it was his first game ever in the major leagues, would be used to pinch-hit. It would be a good way to get Paul's feet wet, so to speak. Besides, just the knowledge that the great Paul Bunyan was sitting on the Cleveland bench would be enough to strike fear into the heart of the opposing team.

And the fans just didn't turn out for the game. They were there for batting practice too. Paul Bunyan taking batting practice! Oh! Wasn't that something to see? Wasn't it?

Of course it was. Every pitch that came anywhere near the plate, why Paul Bunyan would just reach out and swat it out of the park. Out of Boston. Out of Massachusetts. Out of the moon practically. As for running the bases, Paul would just take one mighty stride and he would be on first base. The members of the old Boston Braves, and I mean players like Fewster, and Burns, and Reichle, and Collins and Harris, they just paced back and forth in the home-team dugout, shaking their heads, and praying for rain.

"Is there a cloud in the sky?" Ehmke, the pitcher asked, wiping the sweat from his brow.

"I don't see no clouds," Pittinger, the shortstop said.

"We gotta get a rainmaker up here real fast," Ehmke said. "Real fast. I don't want to get my head knocked off."

"I got a splitting headache," the manager said. "I'm going to go lie down."

"Listen to that breeze," Collins, the center fielder for the Braves said to his downcast teammates. "That breeze means rain. You can't have a breeze like that without a heavy rain running on its heels."

"That's no breeze," Burns the first baseman said. "That's just the stir created every time Paul swings his bat. When Paul comes to bat, they're going to have to tie the catcher and the home plate umpire down, or they're just going to be blown away."

"No umpire, no game!" Ehmke exclaimed, his face brightening.

"Maybe we can score enough runs so that it doesn't matter what Paul does when he gets up to bat," Shanks, the third baseman said.

"That remains to be seen," Pittinger replied, taking up his glove, and running onto the field.

When the organ player struck up "The Star Spangled Banner," the standing-room-only crowd sang it with such gusto that Paul, standing on the field with his cap over his heart, began to weep. And then when the anthem faded, a mighty cheer went up, and the game got underway. Every fan in the stadium was just waiting for the mighty Paul Bunyan to come to bat.

Now if you are a student of the great game of baseball, you can study the box-score of that July game, but you won't find the name of Bunyan anywhere in the line-up. There will be Jamieson and Summa and Speaker and J. Sewell and Lutzke, etc., but Paul's name isn't on the list. Here's why:

In the first inning, Jamieson singled through the hole between third and shortstop, Summa (who was playing right field for the Indians) drew a walk, and then the immortal Tris Speaker doubled high off the wall, and the Indians took a one-to-nothing lead. And then Ehmke settled down. (After all, we can only imagine what was going through his mind when he first took the mound. Between pitches he would just look up and study the least little fluff in the sky, praying that it would be a storm cloud bringing forty days of flood to the land of the bean and cod.) He struck out the next three batters in order.

The score stood one to nothing until the bottom of the fourth. In the home-half of that inning, the Braves gave their die-hard fans something to cheer about. They got to the Indians pitcher (Edwards) pretty good, and, by the time the dust settled, four Braves had crossed the plate.

"Bring up Paul," the fans started to chant at the top of the fifth (and even the Braves' fans took up the cry because they just wanted to look at the man), but the Indians' manager, who felt that he owned the entire world, who felt that he could take the sun and other stars and put them into his back pocket without burning a hole in his britches, just paced back and forth, back and forth, smiling like a cheshire cat. "There's a time and a place for everything," he said, not unlike a preacher administering benediction. "We're going to save Paul for the right game-winning moment. After all, we're not just talking baseball here. We're talking about theater. We're talking the history of the whole world."

The Indians, every last man of them feeling confident, whooped and hollered their teammates on, but there was no further scoring until the top of the eighth. It was then that the Indians got back into the game. Sewell tripled and Lutze sent a long fly ball to the right field. Flagstead got a jump on it and went all the way to the wall to haul it in, but the sacrifice allowed Sewell to amble home. Four to two. Then the Indians walked, singled, clawed, stole, scrambled, bunted, and prayed, until they closed the gap to one. Four to three. Then Edwards took the mound again and didn't give up a run. Thus, the stage was set for the top of the ninth. A pinch-hitting chore was in the wind and the fans knew it. The chant went up. "We want Paul. We want Paul. We want Paul." It went up from the bleachers. It went up from the box seats. It went up from the reserve seats. It was a hymn. It was a prayer. It was a plea. It was a supplication. The rafters shook. The girders grumbled. The suburbs of Boston echoed: "We want Paul. We want Paul." It seemed as if the summer light in the sky parted to take in the words. The paltry score of the game was being transcended.

And so what was meant to happen finally happened. It was one down, and Brower drew a walk (and Ehmke glared at Holmes who was umpiring behind the plate) and Knode, the first baseman, singled, sending Brower to third. O'Neil, the catcher, came up, but O'Neil, no relation at all to the great playwright Eugene, went down swinging. Edwards, the pitcher, was scheduled to bat, but everybody in the stadium knew that there was no way that Edwards was ever going to get to the plate. If anyone besides Paul Bunyan was going to be sent up to bat for Edwards, there was going to be a lynching, a barn burning, havoc in the streets. And a sudden stillness came over the game. And then the announcement was made over the loud speaker: "Batting for Edwards, Number 302, Paul Bunyan." Paul had been given the number 302 because single and double digits looked pretty paltry on such a huge back.

And then the stillness was broken. A cheer went up. And there was Paul standing in the batter box, swinging away, smiling, feeling the power and the glory of the game descending upon his shoulders. Holmes, the home plate umpire, took out his whisk broom and gave the plate a thorough sweeping.

And oh the dreams that floated through Paul's head. He spread his legs to balance his weight. He glared at the pitcher. He wiped the sweat from his face.

"We want a homer!" the fans chanted. "We want a homer!"

Paul nodded. He was prepared to grant the fans their fondest wish. With one swish of the bat, the game of baseball would be changed forever. "I'm going to hit a home run," Paul announced. He pointed toward the center field fence.

"Not with that bat," the umpire said. He stopped sweeping the plate and stuck the whisk broom in his back pocket.

"What?" Paul asked, shaking his head just to make certain that he had heard correctly.

"That bat you have in your hand is not a regulation bat."

"But I made it myself. It's the bat I've been using."

"Sorry, Paul," the umpire said. "Go pick yourself out another bat."

"But I can't hit with another bat!" Paul protested.

"I'm sure someone mentioned to you about the bat," Holmes said, looking at his watch. The fans, sensing something was going wrong, were beginning to get restless.

"No one said anything to me," Paul said. He looked around him for help. Soon the Cleveland Indians team was all over the field, yelling and shouting. The fans started to boo.

"Throw the bum out," the manager of the Braves called. "He's holding up the game."

"You can't do this to Paul Bunyan," the manager of the Indians shouted. His face was bright red.

"What do you mean I can't do it?" Holmes shouted back. "I've got the rules right here. Don't you guys ever read the rules?"

"You can't expect Paul Bunyan to hit with an ordinary bat."

"They haven't changed the rules, have they?" The umpire and the Indians' manager were standing head to head, toe to toe. "Official baseball bats must not measure more than two and three-quarter inches in diameter and must be no more than forty-two inches in length."

"Let me tell you what you can do with those rules!" the manager shouted, and he stepped on the umpire's toes. With pain on his face, Holmes took one step backward and jerked his thumb into the air. "Yer out of this game!" he cried. "Take a walk. Go to the showers. Just don't show your face around here until the final out has been made."

The fans booed. In the meantime, the Indians' bat boy brought from the dugout a regulation size bat. It looked like a toothpick in Paul's hands. He turned to the umpire. "I can't hit with a little-bittie toothpick like this," he said.

Holmes jerked his thumb into the air. "Yer out of this game!"

"Go home, Bunyan," the Braves team called. "Go back where you came from!"

"But I didn't do nothing," Paul replied.

"You say another word, you'll be fined $50 a syllable."

"Take a walk, Bunyan," the Braves cried.

Paul hung his head in shame. In front of thousands and thousands of people he had been humiliated. He had never been treated this way in his own lumber camp. He vowed that no one would ever treat him that way again.

Holmes turned toward the Cleveland Indians' bench. "You had better get a player to bat, or I'll be forced to call a forfeit."

The Indian players merely sat in the dugout and were dumbfounded. They stared ahead with glazed expressions. A few broke down and wept. In an effort to keep the game alive, Gardner jumped up, grabbed the bat Paul had let drop, and ran toward the batter's box. He topped a feeble ground ball toward the pitcher's mound and Ehmke tossed him out. Not that anyone cared. The outcome of the game was not the most important business of the day. In an angry frenzy, thousands of fans spilled out of Braves' stadium and rallied in the streets. The fans demanded the immediate resignation of the baseball commissioner. They wanted the rules changed so that a giant like Paul Bunyan could play with his own bats.

But, of course, the rules were never changed. Not that it would have made any difference to Paul. He was broken-hearted. He trudged back to the clubhouse, took off his uniform, packed it, took a shower, and left the ballpark. He caught the first train back to the Old Home Camp, and he never played baseball again. Not even pick-up games with his own loggers. His uniforms were sold to a circus owner who managed to stitch them together to form a circus tent. As for the bats . . . well, Paul burnt them all. It was quite a blaze, and the fire raised the temperature several degrees. That's why August was so hot that year. It was a world record. A world record.

As for that game in July, Ehmke pitched his heart out, but the Braves lost. The Cleveland Indians, you see, angered that Paul had been thrown out of the game before he had even been credited with an official plate appearance (and that's why his name doesn't appear in any of the baseball record books), decided that they had to win it to avenge Paul's honor. They scored the go-ahead run in the top of the eleventh. Ehmke gave up a walk to take Lutzke home. Then Morton was brought into pitch (since Edwards had been lifted for a pinch-hitter) and held the Braves scoreless in the home-half of the eleventh.

I only tell you all this, you understand, just in case anyone asks.

Johnny Inkslinger Considers the Glory Days
of Cool Papa Bell

In the sweet bye and bye,
Only black players are allowed to take the field,
Whites must watch, perhaps keep score,
While I drive up in my jalopy & leap out.
"Whatjoo want white boy?" they ask,
"You don't drive no car onto the field with us."
"I want to cover the games &
Make you immortal, especially Cool Papa Bell,
The Black Babe Ruth."
"Shoot, boy, don't you know nothing?
We were immortal from the very first,
Immortal because we cd. do something
No white man cd. find it in his heart to do."
Putting away my notepad & pen,
"What's that?" I asked.
"We studied the game to perfection
When there was no hope
Of ever being given a chance."

Johnny Inkslinger Sits in John O'Donnell Stadium in Davenport, Iowa, and Contemplates His Failure To Reach the Major Leagues

☛

What? Shall I remain in the minor leagues forever?
Root for the Quad City Angels
Under a harvest moon too far out of the strike zone?
Don't you think I should like to make it to "the show"
Where salaries have *mucho* zeroes in them, &
The meal money is very generous &
Hotel bathrooms don't sport mildew on the tiles?
It's not that I have made a mess of my life.
Many have done worse. Perhaps I lack conviction,
Wd. not place the neck of the world in a noose &
Pull it tighter. So you hit .250 forever.
Does that mean no *naches* for the left fielder,
That I shall be farmed out to Namaqualand
Where no sportswriter will ever spell my name correctly?
Those are the breaks, kid.
Round men, choking on their cigars, emerge from their high-priced suites
To tell you that you've been traded or let go,
Sent down to British South Africa, to stadiums that no longer exist.
Even if you build, He will not come!
Put behind you, kid, days of whine and ruses, &
Confront the naked truth:
Your life did not work out the way you expected.
In real life, no one pinch hits for you.
In real life, no one comes in at the bottom of the 9th to relieve.
That's the difference between baseball and real life.
Even in the minor leagues.

So What Do You Do if You're a Ball Player and There's No Place Going To Let You Play Ball? You Turn to a Life of Crime. That's What You Do.

℞

Doughnut Hole Harry. What a flood of memories that brings back. Not to you perhaps. But any avid follower of the Canton Tigers, Mobile Oilers, or the Charlotte Whips or any of those other short-lived Minor League miracles might well break down and weep at the mere sound of the name. Doughnut Hole Harry McGraw.

I was stranded in Buffalo, New York, the night of the big blizzard, just sitting around one of the local bars for which that town is so justly famous, nursing my vodka martini like an old veteran and feeling sorry for myself, thinking that maybe selling food processors isn't all that it's cracked up to be, when this old geezer down the bar starts jawing at me. What with the snow falling, one thing led to another, and soon he tells me that he's Doughnut Hole Harry McGraw. Well, you could have knocked me over with a swizzle stick.

Of course, he didn't just come right out and tell me that he was Doughnut Hole Harry. All he said was that he was Harry McGraw and that he had been a ball player once, and so I put two and two together. When I told Harry that my old man—Flakey Davis—used to play third base for the Charlotte Whips back in the infamous '41 season, his eyes turned all watery and he warmed up right away, clapping me on the back, and buying me a drink like I was an old friend or something. "Flakey Davis's kid! You don't say." Actually I did say, and soon Doughnut Hole was telling me the story of his life, which I knew some of it anyway.

More than once I heard my old man talk about this here player named McGraw who once pitched for the Canton Tigers but who went on a bender and missed two crucial games. The manager of the Tigers was so steamed that he decided then and there that he wanted no more to do with McGraw, even if he were leading the league in strike-outs and ERA. Corbett Wilson—I guess he was the manager of the Tigers then—was so steamed that he walked onto the field, crossed over to where the owner of the Mobile Oilers was sitting, and he says, "You want McGraw? Take him. I'm fed up with that S.O.B. I got more important things to worry about than a pitcher who can't hold his booze." The offer kinda took Stoney Norton off guard, but he was quick enough. "What do you want for him?" said Stoney, chewing away on a doughnut. "What have you got?" asked Corbett. "Just this box of doughnuts here," answered Stoney. "Good enough for me," said Corbett. Stoney's jaw dropped opened like he was trying to swallow a dinosaur, but he didn't say nothing. He tossed his half-eaten sinker into the box and pressed the doughnuts into Corbett's hands. And that's how it was done. Corbett Wilson actually traded away his star pitcher for a box of doughnuts. And they weren't even jelly doughnuts at that.

As you can imagine, getting traded to the Mobile Oilers for a box of dough- nuts can put a dent in your life. It put more than a dent into Harry's life. It wrecked his career. No doubt about that. He just fell apart, and he was never stuck together all that good in the first place. He tried to finish out the season with the Oilers, but everytime he would step onto the playing field, fans would pelt him with doughnuts. Fans in the Carolina League are not all that generous— I know because my old man took his share of lumps when his bat went dead—but that's the way they are, and nothing is going to change them. You know, if you've been on the road trying to sell food processors to people who don't know how to boil water, that human nature isn't all that good in the first place. Any- way, poor Harry went from being a 17 game winner to becoming a zilch. He gave up more gopher balls than any pitcher in the history of the minor leagues, and soon he was out of work, sitting in the bus stations of several cities and playing the pinball machines as if his life depended upon it. Perhaps it did, for all I know.

So what do you do if you're a ball player and there's no place going to let you play ball? You turn to a life of crime, that's what you do.

The trouble was that Harry had no better luck in crime than he had on a ballfield. This is some of what he told me in Buffalo while the sky was turning inside out:

"Once I decided on a life of crime, I decided to start small and gradually work my way up to bars and banks. For my first try at the new career, I took a car out of a parking lot behind the bus station, wrapped a burlap sack around the license plates, and stationed myself at a bend of deserted road that led down from Lobolly to U.S. 1. I had been scouting the place for awhile, and I knew that Elmer Davis lived there."

"Elmer Davis?" I asked. "*The* Elmer Davis?"

"Not *the* Elmer Davis," Doughnut Hole said, looking slightly annoyed at my interruption. "I'm talking about the Elmer Davis who managed the Red Apple Super Market. I knew he used to carry around a pretty fat wallet, especially on nights when he was going to play poker, and so when I saw him coming up Lobolly Road, I pretended I was working on my car and that I needed some emergency help. Well, he stopped and when he got out, I pulled my piece on him. That really set him back on his heels. My face was covered with a red bandanna because that's how I seen them do it in the movies. I shot out all of Davis's tires, and then I took his wallet, jumped into my car and burnt rubber all the way down the hill. For a first-timer, I was pretty proud of myself. Nobody was going to catch me and when I counted the money, that wallet contained all of two hundred dollars. Two hundred dollars used to go pretty far in those days, I can tell you that."

I nodded in agreement. One of the hookers was putting money into the juke box and giving us the glad-eye, but we didn't pay her no mind.

"Of course I never spent a cent of it," Doughnut Hole continued, ordering another round.

"Why not?" I asked, thinking how peaceful life could be if you could just stay inside bars and listen to people tell you the stories of their lives.

"What I hadn't counted on was my own wallet. It seemed that when I was fooling around with the car, it must have dropped out of my own back pocket. It didn't have no money in it, but it had enough identification in it to choke a jack-rabbit. The cops were sitting on my front doorstep before I even got home."

"That was tough luck," I said.

"You can say that again. It was more than tough luck. It landed me in prison for a seven year stretch."

"Wow," I whistled.

"More than 'Wow.' More than 'Wow.'" Doughnut Hole Harry stretched out his skinny arms as if he were showing me a fish he had caught. "Of course it did solve some problems for me," he said. "I didn't have to worry about food and lodging for seven years. If I had been left alone out on the streets all that time who would have known what would have happened to me. Besides, the prison had a fair-to-middling baseball team, and I pitched a couple of good seasons up there. At least nobody was tossing doughnuts at me and calling me names.

"One night there was an extra-inning game between the guards and us, and our first baseman Coca-Cola Malone hit a high and fast one over the concrete wall. I wasn't pitching that night, so one of the guards suggested I go look for the ball, because the game can't continue 'less they get the baseball back. As the Warden used to say, he was running a prison and not a summer camp. 'Hey, Harry, go get the ball,' the guard says, and so I say what the hell. I've been a good boy all those years, so why shouldn't I go get the ball. He plops a flashlight into my hand, and two guards open up the gate, and off I go, hotfooting it into the field. The field didn't have much grass in it, but it did have a mess of old tires in it and a ton of broken glass, and there I find the baseball nestled in some weeds, and when I pick it up, something snaps in me. I'm not going back in there, I think. I'm going off to the big city to make my fortune, and so I just kept running. The guards were really pissed, not just because I made them look stupid, but because they didn't get the ball back, and there they were down by one run with a half-inning left to go. That's one thing about baseball games in prison, one thing you can always count on. The guards are always going to name themselves the home team. The inmates, in their eyes, they're just visiting. You can be there for life, but you're only just visiting."

All the time Doughnut Hole Harry talked, I studied his steel-gray eyes and the lines around his mouth. He didn't smile. He didn't laugh. He was just an old man all wound up, an old man with big ears, a red nose, and a hang-dog look that made you want to reach for your wallet and give him a dollar. But this time, because he had known my old man, he was buying, and I wasn't going to keep him from it.

"What happened then?" I asked him.

"When?"

"After you escaped." I glanced out the plate glass window and the sky was all white. The music on the juke box was "Easter Parade." Sometimes, I swear, hookers have no taste.

"Oh, that." He rocked uneasily back and forth in his chair. "My cellmate had some family in New York, so I lit out for there. I ended up repairing pinball machines in Brooklyn for awhile. I thought a lot about getting a job around the ballpark, but I gave it up. I couldn't see rubbing more salt into my wounds than I could handle, so I decided to expand my horizons and embark upon a self-improvement program."

"A self-improvement program?"

"Yeah." Doughnut Hole Harry took off his cap and placed it on the counter. His head was completely bald. I mean completely. It was as if he had shaved every hair from his head.

"What did you do?" I asked, trying not to stare at his head. "You go back to school?"

"Naah. I decided to hold up a bank on Flatbush Avenue. The only reason to go to school is to get more money, right? So why go to school if you can go straight to the bank?"

How could I argue with logic like that? The bartender tossed a funny look our way. I guess he was listening to what Doughnut Hole Harry was saying. I sat back on my chair and noted gravely. Doughnut Hole signaled for another round.

"I had given the bank quite a study," he said. "It wasn't a big bank, but what did I need a big bank for? Even a little bank has got quite enough money for me. It's like searching for women with big tits. How much tit does a man need?"

I nodded. It was a philosophical question that I didn't have no good answer to.

"I decided that I needed two partners. Actually one partner to go into the bank with me and keep the people covered, and just someone to drive the get-away car. You just want to run out of the bank, hop into a car, and go. A bank robber can't stand around and wait for a taxi."

I nodded. The more I drank the more everything in life made perfect sense to me. Everything but food processors.

"Well, friends of a friend had a nephew named Eddie. Eddie was just a seventeen year old punk, but I wasn't asking for an Einstein. I just needed some-one behind the wheel, and so I took Eddie on, though he was always chewing gum and reading science fiction. He had this thing for science fiction. I don't know why. Some kids are just made that way. Anyway Eddie needed the money, and when I offered him three bills just to drive my car, his eyes nearly popped out of his head. Nobody had offered him three bills for anything before. You could tell he was really eager to go with me. Too eager I guess. Christ, that kid would have done anything I asked him. For days he just followed me around like I was the Second Coming.

"The other guy I took on was Jerry Galento. A lot of people called Galento The Eraser because he was good at erasing people, if you know what I mean."

I nodded. I knew what he meant.

"Of course, I was afraid that Galento might get trigger-happy, but those are just some of the chances you got to take. Robbing a bank ain't button, button, who's got the button? You dig? The bank was just a little job, but I thought with any luck I could come away with twenty grand. Twenty grand would have done my heart good right then, I could tell you that. It's more than I'd ever make pitching for the Carolina League. You dig?"

I dug. I couldn't wait to get to the phone and call my old man and tell him who I had run into to, in Buffalo of all places no less.

"I got some gorilla masks from a novelty shop. Oh, I had the whole thing planned out to perfection. We'd arrive early, get the manager as he's going inside, because the manager was always the first one to arrive. Then me and Galento would get all the employees as they entered one by one. We'd wait for the safe to open, take out the money, put the employees inside, and we'd be gone before the first customer arrived. Everything was perfect except for one small miscalculation. One little slip-up."

"You dropped your wallet again?"

Harry took out a red bandanna and blew his nose into it. I wondered if that had been the same bandanna he had used on his first robbery, but I didn't ask him because I didn't want to get his mind off the track.

"I didn't carry no wallet with me on that day," he said. "I had learned my lesson the first time."

"So?" I was surprising myself. I had been raised in a pretty religious atmosphere, but here I was, sitting in a bar and rooting for this crook to get away scot-free. But, maybe, that's the way we all feel about banks. Bank robbers, provided they don't shoot anybody, are all heroes in my book.

"Galento and I get all the employees stuffed into the vault like we was working for a sardine factory, and we got two satchels filled with money. We break for the door, leap into the car, and we're off. I tell you, there's nothing in a baseball game, any baseball game, to compare with that feeling."

I shook my head as if I knew.

"'Step on it,' I yell at the kid, just like we were in the movies. I can see that the kid is as white as a sheet and his hands are shaking. I had driven the car up and had left just a couple of feet from the bank's front door. The kid had slid over and had taken the wheel, and I don't think he had let go of the wheel the whole time that Galento and I had been inside the bank. It was like rigor mortis had set in.

"'What the hell's wrong with you?' I asked him. For an answer, the kid just keeled over onto the front seat. The kid had fainted dead away. Well, Galento didn't waste no time. He jumped out the back, jumped in the front, and took charge. He promptly threw the car into reverse and crunched the back bumper against a Cadillac parked behind us.

"What are you throwing it into reverse for?" I yell at him, but then I figured he was just as rattled because for all we know the kid in the front seat might have died of a heart attack. It's a sure sign that it's not going to be your day when your getaway driver falls apart on you. Well, anyway, Galento finally gets the gears straightened out, but now he's backed down onto a one-way street going in the wrong direction, cutting across traffic. The guy is driving like a madman, which he surely was, and then it dawned on me like a ton of bricks. I had never seen Galento drive before. Eraser had never driven a car in his whole life. When he side-swiped a parked car, I could see the handwriting on the wall. The right-hand door was crunched in, so I couldn't get it open if I had wanted to.

"Galento kept the car going though. I tried to lean across the seat and take the wheel from him, but Galento wasn't having any of my help, and then he hit two more parked cars. I mean I could understand him hitting a moving vehicle. I could probably even forgive him for that. But to hit three parked cars, not even counting the Cadillac, why you'd have to be a complete idiot to do that.

"So there I was, wedged in between two parked cars. I wish I had a picture to show you, because you wouldn't believe it in a million years the way Galento snuck our car in between two parked ones, and my whole life, such as it was, was flashing before me, you dig? Then Galento grabs the satchel and flings open the front door and makes a dash down an alley. I could hear the police sirens wailing not far behind us, and I got this dead kid in the front seat and I got a satchel of bills in the back seat with me, but I can't get out the back doors because by now the doors are crushed in. I tried to climb over the front seat, but then I looked down on that young punk's face, and I knew the jig was up. Even if I could get away, I'm going to leave behind the kid, and that's worse than a wallet, I can tell you that."

"What happened to Galento?" I asked.

"Him going down the alley was the last I saw of him. Maybe he changed his identity and got a whole new life. What the hell do I know? It's hard enough to keep track of my own life, let alone me keeping track of everybody else's. You dig?"

I mulled that over for awhile. Harry put down his beer and excused himself to the Gents; I sat and waited for him. I watched the snow falling in a steady stream, and I felt pretty cozy about my life. It sure seemed a helluva lot rosier than Doughnut Hole's. Anyway I must have waited about twenty minutes or so, and so I went back to the Gents to see if Harry was all right, but when I went into the Gents he wasn't there. Just to be safe, I went into the Ladies as well, figuring Harry might have got them mixed up, but he wasn't there either.

"You looking for your pal?" the bartender asked, looking up from dish-washing.

"Yeah."

"He walked out the back door about twenty minutes ago."

"In this weather?" I asked him.

The bartender, who was just a kid with a lot of long hair, shrugged: "It takes all kinds," he said.

"It sure does," I agreed. "I thought he was buying the drinks."

I paid the bar bill and managed to trudge back to my hotel for the night. It wasn't much of a room, but my mother said I wasn't born to live in a palace anyway.

The next morning I called my old man the first thing. I couldn't wait to tell him about my meeting with Doughnut Hole Harry, and my old man, who retired to St. Petersburg after my mother died, said, "What are you talking about? Doughnut Hole Harry died in prison about five years ago."

"You sure?" I asked.

"Of course, I'm sure," my old man said. He was annoyed because I caught him as he was going out the door to a softball tournament. My old man just loved those softball tournaments. "I read all about it in *The Sporting News* some years back."

"Then who was I talking to?"

"How in the hell do I know?" My old man was also annoyed because he doesn't like talking about friends of his who are dead. At his age who can blame him?

"Tell me. Did Doughnut Hole ever pull a bank job?"

"Yep. Sure did. In Brooklyn. He got caught though. Got caught once before in North Carolina."

I was paying for the phone call, but I kept my old man on for quite a while, trying to get the story straight. Everything the guy at the bar had told me was straight out of Doughnut Hole Harry's life.

"But why would anybody want to impersonate a loser like Harry?" I asked.

"Beats me, son," my old man said. "Now can I get to the game?" With that he hung up. I called my old man back right away.

"What now?"

"What color were his eyes?"

"Whose?"

"Doughnut Hole Harry's."

"How in the hell do I know? I don't even remember the color of your mother's eyes." And then he hung up again. I didn't call him back because I couldn't afford to. I trudged back over to the bar, practically wading though snow up to my waist, but there was nobody there. Now why would anyone pretend to be Doughnut Hole Harry? It doesn't make any sense to me, especially when you could pretend to be a real star.

The next day I called my old man collect, but he didn't accept the charges, and so I just dropped the whole thing. Maybe if I get over to Sing Sing, I'll go look up Harry's grave and see for myself.

Making Baseball Interesting

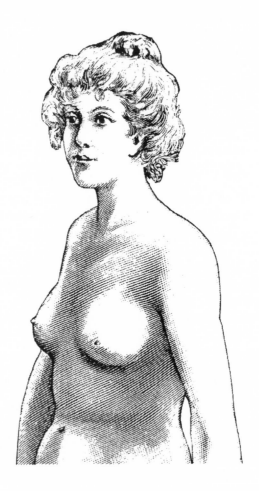

Section 8: Rule 12-A
If a naked woman comes to bat as a pinch-hitter
in an odd-numbered inning, she shall automatically
be awarded first base—if the team at bat has
already made two outs.

What It Is Like To Be a Boston Red Sox Fan

↜

As I sit at my typewriter, the Boston Red Sox are playing the White Sox on television. It is the bottom of the third, with Chicago coming to bat, and Boston is leading 8 to 0. The trouble, of course, is that when the Red Sox play, an eight run lead is nothing. Why, Boston could be leading 20 to 0, going into the ninth, and no Red Sox fan in his right mind would think of making a bet on them to win.

Case in point, Boston once had five full-time .300 hitters in their line-up, and they still weren't able to capture the pennant. Case in point, how many teams can you think of that have lost the only one-game play-offs ever held in American League history? How many teams have lost the pennant on the final game of the season so often? If you're not a raving lunatic at the start of the season, you certainly will be reduced to complete utter madness long before the season is over. Those bums have lost games in ways that have not even been thought of yet. Certainly the Cards have had their Gas-House Gang, and the Dodgers had such characters as Babe Herman, but only the Bosox test a baseball fan to the depths of her or his soul. There are no atheists in the Fenway bleachers.

Some sportswriter has said that rooting for the Red Sox is like taking a roller-coaster ride. Yeah. It's like taking a roller-coaster ride off a cliff. Rooting for the Red Sox is akin to being one of Job's comforters. You talk until you're blue in the face and then God comes out of nowhere and yells at you. There are rumors that the Vatican is going to approve a patron saint for Red Sox fans, give us little plastic statues of a saint striking out—something we can easily attach to the top of our baseball caps—but nothing has come of it yet. Perhaps next season. Red Sox fans thrive on two seasons: the one that has just passed, and the one that is coming up. The season that is going on now is one long blur of agonies and ecstasies.

Case in point, I refer you to the experiences of Lebanon Bashmi. Mr. Bashmi was a thirty-seven year old Arab who lived in my mother's boarding house on Commonwealth Avenue. Although born and bred in the Middle East, Mr. Bashmi had grown to love baseball, baseball in general, and the Boston Red Sox in particular. Watching Mr. Bashmi sit before his portable radio, his head bent to the Red Sox announcers, his hands grasping a bottle of Wild Turkey—well, it was enough to strike terror in a young man's heart.

I was all of twelve years old when Lebanon Bashmi walked into my mother's boarding house, examined the rooms with microscopic interest, nodded his head, and moved in. Mr. Bashmi, as my mother taught me to call him, was a stout man with black hair and eyes that made me feel he could see through lead. He dressed in a white flowing robe, his head covered with a burnoose. He was a brilliant young student, enrolled in the economics program at Harvard. At least that's what he told my mother and my mother had no reason to doubt him, although, case in point, Mr. Bashmi hardly ever left his room. He usually slept during the day and listened to the ball games at night. Fenway park was not far away, but he never went. He preferred to listen to his heroes win and lose over the radio. "I can imagine them," he told me. "I can see all the action in my mind's eye. It's much better than sitting in the stands and having people spill beer all over you."

The word *fan* is merely a shortened form of *fanatic*. Mr. Bashmi was no fan; he was a full-blown fanatic. He recited batting averages and home run percentages, won and loss records. He kept a scrapbook of box scores neatly clipped from the *Boston Globe*. Because I too was a Red Sox fanatic, Mr. Bashmi shared his treasures with me, allowing me to visit his room and to listen to his radio and to dip into his scrapbook. If a player had done particularly well in a game, the player's name would be underscored in red ink and there would be notes written in the margin. Some of the notes were positively cryptic and made no sense at all to my twelve-year-old way of looking at things. One newspaper clipping recorded the salary negotiations of some super star, and under it, in a small, neat hand, Mr. Bashmi scrawled: *"A man, any man will go considerably out of his way to pick up a silver dollar,"* Thoreau.

Not counting my allowance of fifty cents a week, I hadn't thought too much about money before. It bought some things; it didn't buy others. After Mr. Bashmi arrived, however, money began to creep into my thoughts quite often. My mother was quite content to have boarders who could pay the rent on time (since our previous tenant, Mr. Samuel Hipp, wrote checks that took more bad bounces than a ground ball hit over gravel), but it was also common knowledge that the Arabs, all Arabs, were rich, very rich. There was no reason for Mr. Bashmi to be any exception. One night, when the Red Sox were pounding out sixteen hits and were crossing home plate in a regular parade (this in itself was outstanding, for the Sox are capable of leaving so many men on base that you think they must suffer from claustrophobia, not ever wanting to return to the dugout), I worked up my courage and asked, "Mr. Bashmi, do you really have a lot of money?"

Mr. Bashmi raised his brown ear from the radio, and flicked a long cigar ash into the green metal ashtray that my mother had so thoughtfully provided. "Why do you ask that, my friend?" he asked, smiling mysteriously. There were times that he had a Mona Lisa quality about him. Maybe all Arabs were like this. "Do you think money means anything to me?"

I squirmed uneasily upon my wooden chair and pounded my fist into my old man's Vern Stephens' infielder's glove. I had done a bad thing. Mr. Bashmi wiggled a long finger under my nose. "A man, any man, will go considerably out of his way to pick up a silver dollar."

"Thoreau," I announced.

My answer took Mr. Bashmi aback. "How do you know that?" Mr. Bashmi's eyes, which were often streaked with red, stared into my eyes. I could smell the liquor on his breath, and knew he was not a happy man. Happy men didn't drink alone, my mother said. Perhaps she was right, but what did she know about happy men? My father hadn't had a happy day in his life.

"You wrote it in your scrapbook," I told him. "You said I could read your scrapbook. Don't you remember?" If I changed the subject, perhaps Mr. Bashmi would forget that I had embarrassed him. We bent our heads to the final inning of the game. The Red Sox, through the help of a home run by Carl Yazstremski, scored two more runs. Mr. Bashmi wrote some figures on a scrap of yellow paper. He slid the paper over to me, his large hairy hand covering the figures. When he removed his hand, I read the figure: $245,000,000.

"What's this?" I asked.

"What do you mean what's this? You asked me if I had a lot of money. That's how much money I have, give or take a couple of million."

"You're kidding," I said. "Nobody in the world has that much money." Mr. Bashmi shrugged and took the paper back, ripping it into tiny pieces. "If you have that much money," I asked, "then why are you living here, like this? Why don't you move to the Ritz-Carlton?"

"A bed is a bed," Mr. Bashmi said, pouring himself a tumbler of Wild Turkey. If my mother knew that he had been drinking in front of me, there would be hell to pay—245 million or no 245 million. I had no idea if Mr. Bashmi were kidding me or not. The Boston Red Sox announcers were giving their wrap-up of the game. One had gone down into the dugout to interview Jim Lonberg. "What will you do with all that money?"

Mr. Bashmi stood up and stretched his tall frame. "Buy the Boston Red Sox. I can't think of anything to buy better than that."

I sat up as if I had seen a ghost. "The Boston Red Sox!" The hairs on the back of my neck stood up. "What are you going to do with the Boston Red Sox?" I looked wild-eyed and must have been half-frightened out of my wits. "What will you do with them when you get them?" Mr. Bashmi was much too passionate to be the owner of a sports team. If a player made an error or struck out in a clutch situation, there would be no telling what would happen. Mr. Bashmi would have had the unlucky player drawn and quartered, his hands and feet sold in the Boston Commons.

Mr. Bashmi flicked off the radio. Without the drone of the radio to fill it, his room was quite empty. "I'll take them back to Kuwait with me."

I jumped from my chair. "Kuwait!"

"Of course. Don't you think the Arabs deserve to have baseball like everybody else?"

"Did I say they didn't?" I was fairly shouting at my friend. "You can have all the baseball you want. Turn the desert into the largest baseball park in the world, but leave the Red Sox alone."

"I like the Red Sox," he said.

"Like somebody else. Buy the New York Yankees, the Baltimore Orioles; buy the Detroit Tigers."

"The Red Sox are a team that has soul," Mr. Bashmi said quietly. "They play the worst and the best. There is no in-between for them. That is the Middle

East way. I shall buy the team and have the franchise transferred to Kuwait. Then with the United States, Japan, and Kuwait all playing ball, maybe for the first time we shall have a real World Series." His eyes, blood-shot as they were, fairly gleamed with his mad plan. "Hand me my dishdasha, please."

"Get it yourself," I said bitterly. "I'm not your slave."

Mr. Bashmi shrugged and grabbed the dishdasha from the bed. "Why are you angry with me? I'm telling you everything you want to know."

"Why am I angry?" I shouted. "You're taking my team away from me, dragging them off somewhere to play in the desert. Do you realize what's going to happen? The batters will get so much dust in their eyes that they won't even be able to see who's pitching."

Mr. Bashmi placed his hands on my shoulders. "Come now, my friend. You think I'll forget you? Why, I'll have you flown over for any game you want. You'll have the best seats in Kuwait Stadium. You can root for the Kuwait Red Sox as well as the Boston Red Sox."

"Kuwait Red Sox?"

"They have the Red Sox already. There's no sense in making too many changes all at once."

"But you never have even seen them play," I wailed. "How can you buy a team that you've never seen play?"

Mr. Bashmi poured himself some more whiskey. "The Red Sox is one team you don't need to see play. They appeal to one's imagination. They cry out to be seen with an inner eye, not with one's grosser senses."

I picked up my father's Vern Stephens' mitt and pounded it hard. I thought I could work out my anger. "Well, you're crazy," I said.

The back of Mr. Bashmi's head snapped back like he was in a car accident. He wheeled, and, tossing his dishdasha to the table, plucked up a curved knife that he had been using for a letter opener. He grabbed my hair and held the knife to my throat. "What did you call Bashmi?" he said with fury in his voice.

Mr. Bashmi wasn't fooling. I could feel the cold steel against my throat. "I didn't mean nothing by it, Mr. Bashmi. Honest. Please don't hurt me. I didn't mean nothing by it."

He relaxed. "I'm not crazy," he said.

"I know." There wasn't much sense for me to yell for help. My mother had gone to see a movie at the Strand, so we had the building to ourselves.

"When I die and go to Paradise, Paradise will look like Fenway Park. The Red Sox will win every game by one run in the ninth inning. They will always be twenty games in first place and when August comes, they won't fall apart like a snowflake in Florida."

You should live so long I thought, but I did not say it. Instead I presented him some facts straight from the *Boston Globe,* facts to keep his mind occupied and off me. "For one thing, Mr. Bashmi, all the teams in the American League would have to approve the transfer. The American League won't let you take the Red Sox to Kuwait."

Mr. Bashmi glowered at me, slapping his moist palm with the side of his knife. "I'll call Kissinger. Kissinger wants my country's good will." I slowly stood up from the chair and edged my way toward the partially opened door. The Red Sox had whipped Baltimore, so the evening hadn't been a complete loss. I slipped through the door, hardly disturbing it, and walked quietly down the stairs that led to the sitting room. I could hear Mr. Bashmi at the door, calling after me. "Don't you worry, Alexander, I can make it happen. Tomorrow I'll call Kissinger. Kissinger will make the Red Sox move. It will be in the interest of world peace. You're lucky I'm not taking the team to Antarctica," he shouted, closing the door upon himself.

Some joke, I thought. My mother hadn't returned from her movie, so the sitting room was empty. It was just as well. I made certain that I was not being followed, then crossed to a tiny music cabinet where I kept a metal box filled with my father's belongings. The metal box and the infielder's mitt were really the only things I had to remember him by. I opened the box and carefully pulled out a small revolver that my father once kept on hand to fend off burglars. Thank God, burglars had never broken in, because my old man would have shot off his own hand with it. I checked the revolver's chamber to make certain it was loaded, and then I pushed the gun into my belt and covered it with my T-shirt. Mr. Bashmi did not have long to live. As a Red Sox fan, it was the very least I could do for the good of my team.

The following morning, Mr. Bashmi didn't come to breakfast. In fact, he didn't venture out of his room the entire day. Since the telephone was in the sitting room, I decided that he hadn't tried to reach Kissinger, unless he wrote a letter and sent it by carrier pigeon. The Boston Red Sox had decamped for Cleveland, and a front page story in the *Globe* noted that Henry Kissinger had flown to Cleveland to receive some national humanitarian award. Where the great events of the Western World are, can the Red Sox be far behind?

I took the paper up to Mr. Bashmi. The gun was in my belt. Mr. Bashmi gave me a feeble 'Come-in,' and when I entered his room, he was packing some of his belongings in a valise.

"Going somewhere?"

Mr. Bashmi nodded. I showed him the paper and tossed the paper to his bed. "Kissinger's in Cleveland, if you're trying to reach him," I said. I had decided to be as helpful as possible.

Mr. Bashmi nodded. "I heard about it on the radio."

"The Sox are playing a double-header tomorrow. You could go over and see them play and possibly meet Kissinger at the same time."

Mr. Bashmi nodded. "That's where I'm going," he said.

Oh boy, I thought. "No kidding?" I had a vision of myself saying, *Oh no you're not,* pulling out my father's revolver, and letting it rip, just the way they do it in the movies. Instead I asked, "Why don't you let me go with you? It's no fun to sit through a game alone."

Mr. Bashmi unplugged his radio and carefully wrapped the black cord around its body. "I didn't think you wanted me to buy the team," he said.

"I changed my mind," I lied. I would have said anything to go to Cleveland with him. My plan was to murder him in Cleveland, because there were fewer things to explain, and I wouldn't have to worry about getting rid of the body. It made perfect sense to me. People probably didn't take murder as seriously in Cleveland as they did in Boston.

"That's our towel," I said. Mr. Bashmi had taken a towel from the bathroom and placed it in his bag.

"I'm coming back," he said.

"So you're really going to see your heroes play at last," I said. "You could have seen them in Boston anytime you wanted to, but, no, you've got to go to Cleveland."

"I'm saving Fenway for the very end of my life," he said.

"So you're really going to Cleveland." I sat on the edge of his bed and pretended to read the paper, but after I had read the sports pages, there wasn't all that much left.

"I'll be back on Monday."

"How are you going?"

He held out his arms to imitate an airplane. "It must be nice to fly to Cleveland to see the Red Sox play," I hinted.

"I have to be able to say that I've seen the Red Sox play."

"You could say that anyway."

Mr. Bashmi placed his valise on the floor. "You expect me to lie?"

I shrugged. After murder, lying didn't seem all that big a deal. "You want some company?" I asked, my heart thumping away.

"Your mother won't let you go," he said flat-out. He held out his hand for the newspaper.

"She will too," I said, "I can go with you to see a baseball game." I stood up with such speed that I dislodged the revolver. It fell from my belt to the floor. I turned my head for fear it would go off, and before I could recover, my friend from Kuwait kicked the gun with his toe. He pushed forward and scooped it up. "What's this?" he asked.

"Give it to me."

He turned it this way and that, examining the chamber. "This is no toy," he said.

"Give it to me." My legs were shaking. I thought that my heart would leap through my chest and flop on the floor like a dying fish.

"Does your mother know you have this?" he asked softly. I could tell he was angry.

"She knows," I lied. "She sent me out with it to kill some rabbits in the garden."

"With this?"

I nodded. It wasn't a very good lie, but I was stuck with it. I placed my hands on my hips and tried to look nonchalant. "Are you going to give it to me or not?"

It was taking all my self-control to keep from crying.

"No," he said. He tossed my father's revolver inside the valise and snapped the cloth bag shut. "If your mother knows about it, I'll give it to her myself."

"You had better not," I threatened.

He stepped toward me and I backed all the way to the wall. I couldn't leave the room without the gun. "What were you doing with the gun?" I had seen the look in Mr. Bashmi's eyes before.

"I was going to kill you with it," I mumbled.

"What? Speak up."

"I was going to kill you with it, you bastard," I shouted.

My words stopped him in his tracks. "What are you talking about? This is your friend Bashmi."

"Some friend. Didn't you put a knife to my throat the other night?"

"When?"

"The other night."

"You're making this all up," he said. "Let's forget all this," he said. He held out his hand, but I didn't take it.

"Give me my father's gun back. It doesn't belong to you. It belonged to my old man."

Mr. Bashmi started to laugh. "Do you think you're the first person ever to try to kill me? Why do you think I stay in this room all the time? You think I like the view? There are more people who want to kill me than you've got fingers on your hands." I thought he was making it all up to impress me, but I wasn't in any position to argue. Mr. Bashmi snapped his valise from the door and swung it around with one hand. He narrowly missed my face. "And let me tell you something, Alexander, when you threaten an Arab's life, you had better go ahead with it, because if you were a few years older, you would be dead by now."

I taunted him. "Go ahead and kill me. Go ahead and kill me." He looked at me long and hard, looked at me somehow as if I had hurt him deeply, but he simply spat on the floor, pushed past me, with his valise on his shoulder, and went out the door. I slid down the wall and sat on the floor, sobbing.

I guess you can imagine how I felt. The Red Sox would soon be sliding head-first into pyramids, and it would be my fault. I had had a chance to save them from a fate worse than death, and I had failed. It was a double failure. If I had failed in Cleveland, at least I would have gotten the opportunity to see a double-header. But to fail in one's own house without getting a chance to fire a single shot, now that was something else again. I understood how the Red Sox felt when they dropped three straight at Fenway.

Of course what I hadn't counted on was Cleveland itself. The Red Sox-New York Yankee rivalry is the greatest in baseball, but mention Cleveland to a Boston fan, and a pail full of bitter memories will slouch out. You'll see a frown longer than US 1. The Indians give the Red Sox conniptions. Maybe it's the climate, or maybe it's the simple fact that anybody from Boston ventures into Cleveland as if each and every player has a train ticket tucked away in his back

pocket and can't wait to get back home. Municipal Stadium gives the biggest
stars the jimjams.

Case in point. That Saturday I hung around the house like I had an albatross
stitched to my underwear. My mother thought I was running a temperature, but I
didn't tell her anything about my run-in with her boarder. I listened to both games
of the double-header that Mr. Bashmi was watching, although I half-expected
the announcers to break in any moment with the news how Kissinger had ar-
ranged the sale of the Boston Red Sox to Kuwait in exchange for a new guarantee
for peace in the Middle East.

The first game started well for Boston, but it certainly didn't end well. The
Red Sox came into the ninth inning with a five run lead, and, with great style,
they managed to blow the game. Cleveland, in the bottom of the inning, sent six
runners across home plate and won 13 to 12. To add insult to injury, the final run
of the game was scored on a wild pitch. It was the kind of game that causes die-
hard Red Sox fans to take up needlepoint or to go running naked in the streets.

The Secretary of State, Henry Kissinger, showed up in time for the second
game, and there was certainly a lot of ballyhoo about that. When I heard Kissinger
was at the game, I felt sick to my stomach. I could just see him and Mr. Bashmi
sitting together in some box seat, talking about old times and deciding which
plane to stick the players on. I couldn't stand it. I couldn't stand the feeling of
utter helplessness. I sat up. I sat down. I paced the room with fury. I stretched out
on the couch. I clenched my fists. I clenched my teeth. I bit my lip. I leafed
through copies of *Boy's Life.* Nothing I did helped. Nothing I did changed the
fate of the Boston team. Nothing I did helped me or the Red Sox. The Red Sox
were so demoralized by that ninth inning loss to Cleveland that they barely
squeaked out three singles, two of them in the infield, and they went down eight
to zip. Candles were being lit in every bar in Bean Town. We had lived through
worse defeats, but no one ever really gets used to double losses. In a free associa-
tion test, say 'Pearl Harbor,' and Fenway Park springs instantly to mind. Or
Boston at Cleveland. Or Boston. The sportscaster made a joke about trading the
Boston manager for a dozen doughnuts. I doubted if anybody would give up a
good box of doughnuts.

I didn't turn off the radio right away. I was too demoralized to move. Being
a Red Sox fan can do that to a person. The traffic jams you hear about in Boston
are often caused by drivers suddenly going into a catatonic state. If Boston fielded
a team at the time of the Tea Party, we would still be paying exorbitant taxes to
the British.

Anyway, I was lying on the couch, savoring the ashes of defeat, allowing
bitter news to wash over my tortured soul, when an announcer broke in with a
newsflash. The Secretary of State, while leaving Municipal Stadium, was shot at
by a deranged Arab. Dr. Kissinger had escaped unharmed, but the Arab had
been caught. His name, well, you guessed it.

I sat straight up as if the couch had been struck by lightning. I was delirious.
I couldn't believe it. I listened and listened. Just to make certain that I wasn't

imagining things, I changed stations and the news was the same everywhere. An Arab named Lebanon Bashmi had taken a pot shot at Henry Kissinger. He had missed by a country mile and was immediately surrounded and hustled off to jail.

My mother entered the room and was shrieking and waving a dish rag. It couldn't have been worse for her if the Russians had landed or if marijuana had been declared legal. We had been disgraced, she cried. The FBI would be pouring through the front door and all of us would be going to jail. We would have to move from the neighborhood, perhaps go to a foreign country. I felt sorry for her, but I was relieved on one count. No one would sell the Red Sox to Mr. Bashmi now. Of course, I was worried. If he used my father's gun to assassinate the Secretary of State, there would be a lot of explaining to do. My mind raced. He stole it. That's what I would have to say, but it was all very confusing to me. After a twin loss by the Red Sox, the world never made much sense, but this was the straw to break the camel's back.

My mother was making me dizzy, turning this way and that. She ran to the television set and turned off the news. We didn't even bother to turn off the radio. Mr. Bashmi's name came at us from all directions. We had a boarder in stereo. "I should never have rented him the rooms," she wailed, sitting down and running the wet dish rag over her forehead. "I knew there was something wrong with him. The way he'd never go to class. The way he'd just sit up there all day in his room. Who knows what he was doing up there?" I felt very feverish, but my mother was distraught. She was on the verge of a heart attack. I was too young to have a heart attack.

On the television, we caught sight of him—our very own Mr. Bashmi in his dishdasha, being led away, in handcuffs, by the secret service agents. We could barely make out what he was mumbling to himself, but it sounded like 'Red Sox, five run lead, blown it,' followed by a hodgepodge of Arabic. The film certainly didn't flatter its subject. Mr. Bashmi appeared grim and wild-eyed, slightly dazed. The reporter said he had been drinking heavily. My mother and I didn't doubt it.

On a later bulletin, a source close to the investigation revealed that Mr. Bashmi had attended both games of the double-header and had gone berserk. That after the final out of the second game, he ran down the runway shouting that he was going to kill himself. When he reached the parking lot, he pulled the revolver to his head, but the gun jammed. In trying to unjam the weapon, the gun discharged and the bullet sped off in the direction of Henry Kissinger who was emerging from the stadium. The source said the story was being investigated. Some persons at the game had heard Mr. Bashmi's suicide threats but didn't take the threats very seriously. Two agents were interviewed about the possibility of a conspiracy.

Even as the agents talked, I knew exactly what happened. Mr. Bashmi should never have gone to see the Red Sox play. He was correct about staying home and imagining the plays and players. And then to see, to actually see the Red Sox drop a game in the bottom of the ninth, after holding a five run lead, well, it must have driven him over the edge. That's what happens to Red Sox fans. It happens to them all the time. All the time. Anyway, when the FBI came around a few hours later, that's exactly what I told them. One of the men on the investigation team was from Springfield, so he understood. He knew what I was talking about. He knew what it was like to be a Boston Red Sox Fan.

Thoughts at the End of the Baseball Season

Let it be. The final standings are chalked,
Champions crowned.
Averages averaged to the fifth decimal place.
Now the season turns its attention elsewhere,
There are other games to play.
The October sky is chilled with indecision.
What do I do now?
I measure my life by deeds unmeasurable,
Incidents as casual as a kiss
From a friend who means well
But does not own your thoughts.
You cannot make people care.
This I have learned.
What more is there to say about my life
But that it costs
More than I am willing to pay.
Down the narrow street a thousand doors
At the same time open & close.
At last it dawns on me. I understand:
I have left too many runners stranded.

The Little Bar at the Corner

⚑

Walking back home from the shoe factory, Rolfe had passed the little bar on the corner of Schermerhorn and Foley more times than he could count. Actually the square brick building which housed the bar was not in a direct route from the factory to Rolfe's home, a brownstone his grandparents had purchased at the turn of the century, but on Friday afternoons, when a Thoreau-like spirit of freedom infused him, when eight o'clock Monday felt light years away, Rolfe Johnson would walk six or eight blocks out of his way, always alone, never with a companion from the factory, and always with the heady feeling that he might roll up his life in a handkerchief and chuck it in an alley somewhere, leaving Eunice and their four children stranded, one more human island of mouths floating on Welfare somewhere in the bowels of the mid-twentieth century.

On the first Friday in June, however, a sign appeared in the window, a cardboard sign announcing that the St. Louis Bar was under new management, but everyone over eighteen was welcome to partake of the air-conditioning, the television set, and of course the liquid refreshment.

Rolfe read the sign twice and then glanced through the window at the customers gathered beneath the television set. He could not help but feel that the televised baseball game was strangely out of place. For one thing, the picture was in black and white. Rolfe didn't think that would be good for business. For another, the players' uniforms were not exactly familiar to him, not that he was an exceptional baseball fan, though he had taken Paul, his twelve-year-old son, to watch the New York Yankees play three or four times. Rolfe was tempted, but he did not enter. A pain spread through his chest.

On the third Friday in June, when Rolfe passed again, the cardboard sign had been removed from the window, and the television set, a twenty-seven inch Admiral, seen clearly from the street where Rolfe stood, his metal lunch pail clutched awkwardly in his left hand, played on. A baseball game. Rolfe glanced at his watch. Six-thirty. Perhaps it was the first part of a twi-night double-header. The uniforms flashed; his curiosity overcame him. Brushing his blonde hair away from his eyes, he turned the handle on the oak door and entered.

The bar was not a long one, eight feet long at most, and the seven black leather stools with backs were taken. A line of businessmen in suits. Rolfe, allowing a few moments for his eyes to become accustomed to the low light, glanced uneasily about him, hoping to see some women. He very rarely frequented bars, and he remembered that one time he had mistakenly entered a gay bar and had to back out quickly, experiencing a marked hostility from the regulars who knew he was an outsider. He was not comfortable in bars in any case. His stern Lutheran upbringing had precluded such enjoyment.

"What'll it be, Mac?" the bartender asked. His tone was friendly. He was a dark-skinned, completely bald man who wore his white shirt with the sleeves rolled back to the elbow.

"A beer," Rolfe answered awkwardly, not knowing if that were the right thing to order or not. Nobody turned around to mark his entrance. All eyes were intent upon the game in progress. Rolfe was relieved to see two women sitting at a table. They were in bright red dresses, low-cut, revealing ample black bosoms. Prostitutes, he thought. Still he found their presences oddly reassuring.

"This is the inning where St. Louis scores three big ones," he overheard the man in the first chair say to one of the women. Without turning his head, the huge man behind him swept a gin and tonic from the bar in a single graceful motion, his great paw of a hand skimming across the bar the way a skater might make a turn on ice. There were no free chairs. Rolfe remained standing.

"Any particular brand?"

"This brings up the National League Batting Champ," the television sportscaster announced. "Stan the Man Musial. Just listen to the crowd. What a season he's had."

The bear-like man in the black suit pointed toward the screen. "Watch this double. What a beauty it is."

"Schlitz," Rolfe ordered. He set his lunch pail on the floor, allowing it to lean slightly against his left ankle, in case anyone would get the idea of trying to steal it.

"Schlitz?"

"If you have it." He wondered what it would cost.

"Dixie Walker's going back, but the ball's by him, it's over his head," the announcer called, his voice rising with the action. "Stan the Man's going for two. Here comes the throw. And he's in there with a stand-up double."

A red-headed woman, six-foot tall, in a black dress, emerged unsteadily from the ladies' room. "One of these nights, Old Dixie's going to rear back and throw it in there and toss him out. You just wait and see." She crossed to a side table and sat down. "You just wait and see," she repeated, holding her compact mirror to her face. She tested her lipstick.

"You wait and see yourself, honey," the blonde man in stool number three answered. "I don't think I can live that long." He chuckled at his own rejoinder and a ripple of laughter passed among the other patrons. Rolfe grinned self-consciously, not quite understanding the nature of the joke. When the bartender set the mug of Schlitz down, he told Rolfe, "Come back tomorrow. Then you can catch the whole thing from the beginning."

Rolfe didn't understand but he nodded. The bartender winked and gave a cryptic smile.

"It looks as if Hatten has gotten the sign to give an intentional pass to Whitey Kurowski."

"Boo." The freckled face man on the fourth stool raised his fingers to his lips and emitted an ear-splitting whistle. Everyone turned and looked. His blue shirt was partially unbuttoned, and the knot in his black tie was pulled halfway down.

"Don't mind him, chum," the bartender said. "He's a Brooklyn fan. There's always one in every crowd." He tapped Rolfe lightly on the arm. Rolfe tried to concentrate on the game.

"Tonight, we're all Brooklyn fans. Ain't that right, Whitey?" a man in a black suit asked. He turned and smiled at Rolfe, but the fancy sunglasses he wore obscured half his face.

"Ball four," the sportscaster said. "And so Whitey gets his first walk of the ball game. So that brings Enos 'Country' Slaughter to the plate with two out and two men on."

Rolfe wondered if the man with the sunglasses could really see the telecast. Weirdos, he thought, but he refused to retreat. He sipped his warm beer slowly, allowing the foam to fleck his mustache. He did, however, promise himself never to return.

"Grady Hatten rears back and fires one in. A fast ball. There's the swing. Oh, did Country have that one perfectly timed. There it goes, deep to right center. It's way over Furillo's head. It's going to be in there for extra bases. Musial's rounding third. He'll score easily."

A black man leaning on the juke box started to applaud. He danced a little dance. "They're waving Kurowski home," the television set said. The man on the second stool chewed his cigar violently and applauded the black man's jig. "Furillo's got the ball. Here comes the peg to third. The slide and Country is in there with a triple." The crowd at the ball park roared hysterically.

The freckle-faced boy stared at the dancer sullenly. "Wait a minute, youse guys," he said at last. "I thought you were rooting for the Bums today."

"If that ball had just climbed a little bit, it would have been out of here."

"Ah, let us alone," the man in sunglasses told him, jabbing his cigar stub into the air to emphasize his point. "What difference does it make who we root for? Huh, wise guy?"

"Hey, Rudi, keep calm," the bartender admonished his customer.

"That makes the score four to one in favor of the Cards."

The boy with the freckled face stood up. The man at the juke box stopped dancing. "Of course it makes a difference. The Bums are a better team."

"Says who," the tall woman said from her table. She had kicked off her blue pumps and sat in her stocking feet, beating time to some imaginary music.

"Look at the line-up. Stanky, Walker, Furillo, Reese." His face puffed red with excitement. He was not reciting names; he was reciting poetry, his own private poetry.

"Look at the other line-up," the black man said.

"A police line-up is the only line-up youse guys understand," one of the women in red added.

The announcer made himself heard above the roar of the crowd. "This brings up Dusak with two outs and Slaughter on third."

A thin pale man, almost sixty years old, and the tallest person in the bar, in fact the tallest person that Rolfe, who stood over six feet himself, had seen in a long time, pointed a shaky finger at the screen, where the picture began to roll. "Tell it to the guy standing on third," he laughed.

"And Hatten the pitcher," the red-faced boy added.

"Dusak scored in the bottom of the first on Marty Marion's sacrifice fly."

Rolfe turned his head toward the old man whose skin was covered with brown age spots. The man's teeth were yellow and jagged, and there were gaps where some had rotted away. They were not human teeth at all, Rolfe thought, and a shiver went down his spine. "Country knows how to hit. God knows that man knows how to hit," he said to Rolfe.

The bear-like man with the gin and tonic shouted at the screen, "Take the bum out. Send him to the showers."

The black man at the juke box tapped his chest several times and shook his yellow shirt. "I'm the one covered with sweat. I'm the one who should be sent to the showers."

"Don't smell too good neither," one of the women added.

"Can it, Sally," the man with sunglasses said. "Or I'll let you have it with the back of my hand." The back of his hand was covered with gray hair.

The bartender attempted to divert attention back to the game. "Watch Dusak stroke this single."

"Yeah, Reese don't have no chance for it. Country is coming home like a cow to the barn." The black man turned his back on Sally and entered the men's room. The bartender slapped at an imaginary fly with his wet white towel and drew another mug of beer from the tap.

Rolfe fidgeted. "What game is this?" he quietly asked the old man on his right.

The old man's lips formed a muted smile. "You've got to be kidding," he said, turning his head back to the screen just in time to see Dusak's single.

* * * * *

Rolfe vowed to stay away from the bar on the corner, but that third weekend in June, when he had driven Eunice and the kids back and forth to the beach, his thoughts were on the Brooklyn Dodgers and the sudden death playoff with the St. Louis Cardinals, back to 1946 and to Stanky, Musial, Reese, Schoendist, Walker, Dusak, Slaughter, and the entire crew of professionals lifted from the past. He concluded that Seidenstein, for he ascertained that was the bartender's name, also the owner of the place, according to the kid with the freckles, had rigged some kind of video tape system to play back old games. Unfortunately old games did not seem to attract the most prosperous clientele. The prosperous ones were in search of something new, Rolfe thought. In fact, the tall geezer with the jagged teeth gave Rolfe the creeps. That Sunday he had dreamt he had doubled off the right center field wall and the man with the sunglasses slid into home with the tying run. When he awoke, the sheets were covered with sweat.

That Monday, immediately after work, Rolfe found himself standing on the corner of Schermerhorn and Foley, staring at a polished padlock. Red checkered curtains were drawn across the window and the doors were locked. Rolfe shrugged it off. Monday was often a dark day for restaurants and bars.

He returned on Tuesday, Wednesday, Thursday, and still the building remained closed. Rolfe peered and peered through the checkered curtains, smeared the plate glass with his handprints, but could make out nothing. His dreams intensified. He was now always up in the bottom of the ninth with the bases full and there were two strikes against him. He began to doubt his own sanity. Perhaps that baseball replay never occurred. Thursday evening he made a few inquiries at the neighborhood newsstand and at a nearby laundromat, but nobody could tell him anything. A woman in slacks, unloading clothes from a dryer, suggested the building had been sold but did not know to whom. On his way out of the laundromat, a freckle-faced cripple, both legs cut off below the knees, handed him a black-bordered card and smiled. Rolfe studied the face carefully to see if it bore any resemblance to the boy at the bar. Could it be his son? He came to no conclusions.

"Do you know anything about the bar on Schermerhorn?" he inquired.

The cripple, rolling forward on his wooden board, turned his neck grotesquely. "The world is coming to an end," he said tapping the card in Rolfe's palm. "Sinner repent. Repent before it's too late."

Rolfe frowned and hurried out, racking his brains all the way home for the terrible sins he had committed.

On Friday, his sense of freedom returned, he doffed his gray uniform, showered, and left the factory in record time. He imagined he felt like a rookie pitcher entering a major league game for the first time. By the time he turned down Schermerhorn, he was out of breath and his hands were trembling. He had run the last two blocks at full speed, but his hunch was right. The padlock was removed, the curtains were open, and there were customers inside. Rolfe pushed the doors open and immediately searched for the women in red dresses. Two women were sitting at the bar, away from the television set, but there was a new bartender. A short fat man with a head of curly brown hair.

"What can I do for you, Mac?"

"What happened to the guy who was here last week?"

"You got a badge?"

"What?" Rolfe felt the sharp pain in his chest.

"Is this an interrogation? You from the police or something?"

Rolfe reddened, and glanced about to gain corroboration. A pain shot through his chest. He recognized none of the faces. The man on the second stool wore sunglasses, but was not the same person from the week before. The women in the green dresses sipped ginger ale through straws, and the television set was on. The ball game was on.

"I'm sorry," Rolfe said. "I was just curious. I'm not from the cops. Honest."

"And that brings up Erv 'Four Sack' Dusak with one out in the second," the sportscaster was saying. "And let me remind you folks at home that it's a beautiful cloudless day here in Brooklyn, with the Cards and the Bums fighting for their lives in this two-game play-off to see who meets the Bosox with their Splendid Splinter in the World Series." There was no video recorder, or at least Rolfe couldn't see one, his blue eyes carefully searching the wires.

The bartender placed a mug of beer in front of his latest customer. "Sit down and make yourself comfortable. Have one on the house in honor of the big game. This is the big one."

"Anyone take the Bums for two-to-one odds?" the man on the first stool asked. His two large fists were stuffed with dollar bills.

"Quit your clowning, Harry," the woman with the ginger ale said.

"Can't you see that the new guy here is having a heart attack?" She turned to smile at Rolfe, to adjust the black corsage pinned to the bodice of her dress. She was a slender woman who wore her blonde hair short and straight. "That Harry's always kidding. This place is full of jokers, isn't it? We get them all eventually, don't we, Rule?" She turned her attention to the bartender, and Rule nodded in agreement. So did Rolfe, just to be friendly.

A pale woman with a patch over her left eye, lightly touched Rolfe on the elbow. "Don't let them bother you. I must have been through this a thousand times, and I never get tired of it. It's a beautiful game, tense and exciting." Rolfe's breath stopped. "Dusak's going to triple here," she continued, not taking her eye off him, "but just wait till you see Slaughter's triple in the fifth. That one will kill you. It's so beautiful. It almost makes me cry."

The possibility of tears falling from one eye turned over in Rolfe's mind. "It's going to the left-field wall," the announcer shouted. No one had to look. No one doubted him. Rolfe picked up his beer, trembling in anticipation. He resigned himself to the fact that there was no video recorder anywhere, but that was all he was resigned to. He couldn't wait for the fifth inning, when Musial would double, Enos "Country" Slaughter triple, and Dusak single Slaughter home. Outside, it was a beautiful cloudless day in Brooklyn and he was free. He had nowhere else to go.

I'm Talking About the '41 Season

ㄹ

Does anybody out there remember the Charlotte Whips? I doubt it. The Whips have been dusted down to oblivion, but then again who or what ain't? Now I'm talking about the Carolina League in the late 30's and the early 40's, when us Whips were top dog, when eighteen or twenty of us—depending on who was sick and who was healthy, or who was in the lock-up and who was being pursued by somebody's old man hell-bent on a shotgun wedding, depending on who was drunk and who was sober, and who was in the manager's doghouse and who was tilting the lumber for a hefty average—when eighteen or twenty of us tore around North and South Carolina, dipping into Georgia and Florida, swinging over to Mobile and Nashville on our rat-trap bus that had no shocks left and made every pebble feel like a boulder and every rut in the road feel like a long descent to you-know-where, playing games as far away as Canton, Ohio. We were getting pretty hard up for Triple A clubs in those days, and of course when the Japs got our piss up, all the healthy players were drafted. Audie Lucretius Ferguson, a thirty-game winner in the 1940 season, was the first from our club to go, and he came back a couple of years later with a pin through his right hip. And then, if I remember correctly, there was Simpson Catwalk who signed up on the day of his 18th birthday. I remember because his ma cried something awful, but it had to be done, and we all knew that, even if we were all worked up about catching the Canton Tigers and putting their asses in a sling. There were a lot more fellas who came and went, but there's no sense reciting all their names, because most of the names won't mean nothing to you anyway. Some of us made it up to the majors for a brief spell, filling in for the regulars until the war ended, but most of us, for one reason or another, didn't. The war did awful things to us, even to those of us who had to stay behind. Maybe especially to those of us who had to stay behind.

Anyway, I'm talking about the '41 season in the Carolina League, a couple of years before most of the minors shut down for lack of players and lack of most everything else. As far as we were concerned, the Charlotte Whips were the cat's pajamas, and we were doing our damndest to take folks' minds off the war. We tried mighty hard, we certainly did.

The season I'm talking about is the time when most baseball fans were concentrating on a young Boston kid named Theodore Samuel Williams, wondering whether he could bat .400 in the big leagues. It was the season that DiMaggio put together his 56-game hitting streak, and so you can see there were a lot of things to think about. Unless you were close to home, the Charlotte Whips were probably not high up on your list of things to worry about.

'41. We had a great team that year, even though our star pitcher, Audie Ferguson, the one I told you about, came down with a sore elbow and could only come through with ten wins for us, against four defeats. Of course, everybody knew that it would be difficult for Fergy to come off a thirty-win season and not feel the pressure to equal or better himself. On the other hand, we really didn't expect to have Fergy at all. A thirty-win season drew a lot of scouts, and Fergy signed with the Cards for a pretty good bonus. Off he went to spring training with visions of the World Series dancing before his eyes. Trouble was that Fergy had an eye for the ladies, and there were rumors that Fergy got himself involved with the wife of one of the high muckamucks. I never got the full story, but sure enough, the Cards sent him back to us for safe-keeping, and the '41 season got off to a splendid start. Fergy pitched a two-hitter on opening day, and by the time July Fourth rolled around we were giving the Canton Tigers a run for the money. Nobody expected the Whips to do so well, least of all us, but there we were, going into the second half of the season, trailing the Tigers by only two games. We knew we had them nailed.

Then Fergy's sore elbow really started acting up. Spike Kellings, our not-exactly-lovable manager, took the grim news as best he could. He broke down and cried like a baby. Then there were a lot of late night confabs with the owner—Sonny Joe Terrel of the Bristol Distillery fortune—and the upshot was that we reached down into Jacksonville and brung up a sunny-faced, peach-fuzzed kid called Slats Hartgrove, a fair-to-middling southpaw, who had smoke on his fast ball, but who would often toss a curve like he was putting wash out on the line. Still, everybody on the team felt that Sonny Joe and Spike had done the best they could under the circumstances. There are worse things in the world than to watch a thirty-game winner go sour, but there ain't too many. Fergy was a hard-luck gent after that, and the war didn't do anything to dispel that notion. Slats was no Fergy, that was for sure, but "Hell," Spike said, "it's better to have somebody out on that mound than nobody at all." If he said it once, he said it a thousand times, especially when we went into a five-game losing streak that nearly dropped us out of contention. "It's better to have somebody out there than nobody at all." It was that sentence that must have gotten him to think about the ghost business, which must go down in baseball lore as one of the great strategies of all time. At least in my book. Before I tell you about the ghost business, I got to fill you in on a few things. First, the members of the Whips, and second, the final situation.

Now, I got a picture of the Charlotte Whips right in front of me, but I don't need no picture to remember the team that year. Spike Kellings, who swore up and down that he wasn't Jewish, was our manager. Boris Carlyle, the Mad Russian, who got his nickname from a radio show, was our catcher. Charlie Malone was at first, I was at second, Flakey Davis at third, Cat Crosby at shortstop. The outfield, which had the tendency to play in too shallow whenever Slats was pitching, consisted of identical twin brothers—Woody and Barry Strode—and Barrett Conley, he was nicknamed The Professor because he was about the only one on the team who had seen the inside of a college. We'd seen him read real books, and not comics neither. It was enough to make you wonder about what life was all about. One day, The Professor came to the ballpark early and I see'd he's reading a book—*How to Win Friends and Influence People,* by Dale Carnegie—so I says, 'That's the kind of book I could use,' real friendly like, and The Professor turned right around and lent it to me. I still have it. I should send it back to him, but he's dead now, so I don't think he'd have much use for it.

Anyway, we had Slats and Fergy and some other guys as pitchers, but the guys I told you about were the real heart of the team, not forgetting 17-year-old Simpson Catwalk, who served as an all around pinch-hitter and general utility man. He was pretty young, but he had a lot of speed. Sometimes it's necessary just to be able to run real fast.

It was right after the Fourth of July when Slats came up from Jacksonville, where he had been playing for some American Legion team. The first thing that Flakey Davis did was to take Slats out to the bullpen and carefully point out where Flakey had planted corn and tomatoes in the bullpen. It didn't seem right to Slats that someone should plant corn and tomatoes in the bullpen, but Slats being new and all, he took the hint and he did all his warming up in the dugout runway, and sometimes right under the bleachers. It wouldn't have done Slats no good to protest, because Flakey was leading the Carolina League in home runs, and nobody, least ways the manager and owner, felt like upsetting him. Besides, when September rolled around, that corn tasted mighty good. I can't speak much for the tomatoes because I didn't get much of them.

Actually, nobody on the Whips got any tomatoes, because Woody Strode— at least I think it was Woody because sometimes he and his brother would switch places and nobody could tell them apart—fell all over them one afternoon when he was in the process of saving the game with a spectacular catch. Woody was left field, and Slats was on the mound, holding on for dear life to a slender 5-4 lead. We were playing the Mobile Oilers and we were on the field at the top of the ninth, when Slats started to get a little wild. In a small matter of nineteen pitches, he managed to get the bases loaded, with two outs, and Bing Dougherty coming to the plate. Bing Dougherty was a terror with men on base that season, but Slats managed to smoke two fast balls by him, and then, on the third pitch, the curve ball got up a little high and a little too long, and Dougherty smashed what looked to me like a sure-fire grand slam. But Woody Strode took off at the crack of the bat, and with his back toward home plate, ran all the way to the little green wall that separated the bullpen area from the rest of the field. Strode leapt into the air, caught the ball, and tumbled right into the bullpen. Nobody knew exactly what happened, but finally Woody stood up and showed that the ball was in his mitt. The umpire called Dougherty out and we won the game, and moved into first place, ahead of the Canton Tigers, who had lost to the Raleigh White Sox.

Frisco Wilson, the silver-haired manager of the Mobile club, took one look at Woody Strode standing in the bullpen and he jumped out of the dugout, screaming and tearing his hair. "He didn't catch that ball," he shouted. "He dropped it and then picked it up and put it in his glove. And if he says otherwise, he's a liar."

Well, Spike stood up and said, "Nobody calls one of my players a liar and gets away with it." In a matter of seconds both benches emptied and there was a donnybrook going on that made Sherman's march through Georgia look like a tea party. Everybody was in on it, everybody that is except Flakey. Our third baseman retreated to the bullpen. He moaned over those trampled tomato plants something awful. I don't believe he said a civil word to Woody the whole rest of the season. Anyway, the umpires had to call in the Charlotte fire department to separate the mass of slugging, bleeding, yelling, and tortured bodies. All of us got hosed down pretty good and soon we were all covered with a layer of mud. Even Flakey's tomato plants got watered, although the moisture came a mite too late. There were so many fines meted out that most of us were eating oatmeal three meals a day for two weeks, and I came away with a shiner that the best steak in town couldn't unswell. But we got credit for the win, and, as I said, that put us one up on the Tigers.

That's the way it went most of the season. We'd win one and climb into first. Then we'd drop a couple, and the Tigers would overtake us. It was a see-saw battle the whole campaign, and so the '41 season came down to our final three games with the Canton Tigers. We dropped the first game when Charlie Malone, our first baseman, struck out with the bases loaded, and then we took the second 9 to 3, when the Strode Brothers and The Professor batted the apple around like there was no tomorrow. I hit a triple myself. So there we were, on the final game of the season, with us and the Tigers having the same identical won and lost records. 61 games won, and 48 lost, with one game left to play. I suppose I should explain that the Carolina League featured a 110-game season then, forty-four games less than the Majors. But, then, the players in the Majors got to travel a lot more comfortable than we did.

Spike Kellings, our manager, was lighting candles in church, praying he could get a couple of pitching innings from Fergy in the crucial series, but it didn't work that way. Fergy's elbow was acting up something awful. And so Spike put the nod to Slats Hartgrove. By that time in the season Slats had settled down real good and had an overall record of 6 and 2 for us, but not even heaven was going to give him a curve ball. If that weren't all, Cat Crosby, our shortstop, got hit by a car while walking to the ballpark and was rushed to the hospital with a fractured leg. Crosby's sideways brush with death didn't make none of us feel too good, but we had the kid to fill in, so Simpson was slated to take over at shortstop.

Not that everything was bad. The Mad Russian had a good book on the Tigers, and The Professor, in spite of all that reading which couldn't have done his eyes no good, was clobbering the horsehide at a .378 pace. Nobody, but nobody was going to catch the Professor for the league lead in batting. And Flakey was leading the league with home runs, having belted 36 out of the park, and I wasn't having too bad a season myself. Not only was I leading all second basemen in the league in fielding percentage, but I was also hitting a career-high of .282, with lots of doubles and stolen bases thrown in. Catwalk led the Whips with stolen bases. He had swiped thirty-two, exactly twice as many as I had managed. But then I was no sweet seventeen.

There was also no doubt that the Tigers had a good team too. Their top hitter was Nero Callahan. Callahan, a first baseman by trade and a center fielder by necessity, was going along at a .357 clip and had hit safely in his last twelve games. In addition, Corbett Wilson, the Canton manager, had saved a pretty fair-to-middling pitcher for the big game. The Tigers' starting pitcher was a sandy-haired southpaw named Rosenthal. Rosenthal not only led the league in strikeouts, but he was sporting an incredibly low 2.46 earned-run-average. There was no doubt that we had our work cut out for us. Most of the local yokels figured Canton to clinch the title, but then they hadn't figured, as nobody had figured, on our manager coming through with a ghost to pinch hit.

The final game of the season, as usual, was scheduled for Labor Day. That's because management could always figure on a pretty good crowd to turn out. It was Labor Day, and it was a hot one. I get beads of sweat just thinking about it. We weren't even into the second inning when the sun was beating down on us like it was going to burn a hole into every living thing. Most of the spectators—and 4,000 of them had crowded into our ballpark that day—had taken off their shirts (the menfolk, that is), and so they were slightly better off than us. There are times in life when it's much better to sit back and watch, rather than have to take part in things. Most of the fans, of course, were just fine, but there are always a few spoiled sports around. One guy in particular, a man with a beer belly and straw hat, kept yelling at Flakey all afternoon. He was riding our third baseman pretty hard, too hard to suit us. When Flakey struck out in the second inning, the guy yelled, "You don't need a bat, Flakey, you need a hoe. How are the crops coming? Whatja goin' to grow next year?" and that sort of thing.

The heckling and the heat must have got to Flakey pretty bad, because in the top of the fourth, after the Whips had taken a one-to-nothing lead, thanks to a stand-up triple by The Professor and a long sacrifice fly by yours truly, Flakey let a ground ball go right through his legs, and Truman "The Ape" Hirsch, the Tigers' brawny catcher, dashed home with the tying run. "Give Flakey a peach-basket instead of a glove," the man in the straw hat shouted, and Flakey turned bright red and not from the sun neither. Even from where I was standing, I could see Flakey grinding his teeth and I could hear him talking to hisself. Sometimes people in the stands have all the advantages. Well, in the bottom of the fourth we didn't come up with no runs, and neither team scored in the fifth. Then, in the top of the sixth, the Tigers started getting to Hartgrove. Callahan doubled off the wall, and then Slats walked Peaches MacAdoo. That was all Spike needed to see. He took Slats out and waved in Russ Oberlin for relief. Slats got a pretty good hand from the crowd, and that felt nice. Russ came on and got the Tigers' left fielder, Don Cranston, to ground into a double play, moving Callahan to third. Then the next batter singled and Callahan scored. Oberlin picked the runner off first, and so the score stood 2 to 1 in favor of the Tigers until we got up in the bottom of the ninth. You coulda cut the tension with a butter knife.

We wanted to win it so bad it hurt. Flakey led off the bottom of the ninth for us, and he decided to get some revenge upon the heckler behind third base. Flakey drew a bead on his man and fouled off eight consecutive pitches, lining each and every foul within feet of the straw hat. Anybody who had seen it would have wrung their eyes with disbelief. It was a tremendous exhibition of bat control, but of course Spike was smoldering, because it wasn't doing nothing to help us win the game. The line-drive fouls sent the heckler scattering for cover. The last we seen of him was him sitting under his seat and not on top of it. Another thing was that all those foul balls was beginning to wear down the pitcher. Rosenthal was still in there, and he hadn't walked a man all day, but those foul balls got to him. He threw four wide pitches and Flakey took his base. We had the tying run on.

The Professor was batting clean-up that day. He dug into the batter's box, took a called strike, and then blooped a double down the left field line. Unfortunately, Flakey had no speed and the ball weren't hit all that good, and so Flakey had to hold at third. Flakey was now back within earful distance of his fan in the straw hat. "Get a horse, Flakey. Get a horse," he yelled. All those foul balls hadn't done what they were supposed to do. I was on deck, waiting for Barry Strode to bat, so I could see Flakey getting hisself all worked up again. Flakey kept pounding his left palm with his fist.

Barry, sweating like a pig, took a mean cut at a low slider. He was hitting .290, with 18 homers, so he was having a pretty mean season. He looked down the third-base line and took a sign from the coach. On the next pitch, a fast ball, Barry laid down a bunt and it spun between the pitcher and first base, catching everybody off guard. The throw to the plate was late, and even so the ball got away momentarily from Truman "The Ape" Hirsch, so Barry was able to go on to second. The Professor, with the winning run, clung to third like the base was a tiny lifeboat.

Flakey got up and brushed hisself off, but I could see right off there was a strange look in his eyes. The Ape was doing a slow burn, but he knew it was a good and fair play, and so there was nothing to be done. The score was now 2-2, and the fans were giving us a pretty rousing cheer. I started up to the plate, but when I glanced back over my shoulder I could see Flakey hot-footing, not into the dugout, but up the third-base line. He jumped over the small barrier that had been erected in front of the good seats. When the man in the straw hat saw Flakey coming at him with murder in his eyes, that guy took off like the devil was in him. Up and down the stands they went, with the fans yelling and shouting and grabbing, and our manager in the dugout groaning, moaning, and cursing, tearing at his hair. Flakey finally cornered the heckler on top of one of the bleachers and really peppered him with the one-two. I tell you the guy went down like a sack of potatoes sliding down a chute. By the time the two cops assigned to that section reached Flakey, Flakey had taken the man's boater and punched his fist through it, leaving it to dangle around the man's neck like a giant doughnut.

Spike was yelling at him and cursing up a storm, but of course it was too late for anybody to do nothing. Flakey was not only ejected from the game by the umps, he was led from the ball park in handcuffs. We could hear the police siren, but we'd scored the tying run. Still, Spike was going crazy. Not only did he not have his best home run hitter in the line-up in case the game went into extra innings, but Flakey's arrest meant that we might have to make some defensive changes. If we took the field in the top of the tenth, Simpson would be switched from shortstop to third, and then Maury O'Neill, one of our rookie reserves, would have to go in at short. Since Maury O'Neill was batting all of .178 for the season, you can guess how thrilled Spike was over the prospect of getting him into the line-up.

It took awhile to get the crowd quiet enough to continue play, but then the uproar started all over again when Corbett Wilson, the Tigers' manager, leapt onto the field to say that Barry Strode, who was dancing around second base, wasn't really Barry Strode at all but was really Barry's twin brother, Woody. That the runner on second, he insisted, then should be called out for batting out of turn, and that the tying run be disallowed, and the runners returned to their bases. Leo McGurk, who was umping, looked pained. Our manager was jumping up and down, all of which we knew was not good for his heart. "Are you out of your mind?" he screamed. He grabbed for Woody Strode and pushed our hapless outfielder forward. Least ways I thought it was Woody. I mean nobody could tell the difference, except for the numbers on their backs, and they could have switched shirts. Also, everybody knew that Woody was an even better hitter than his brother and that their batting stances were slightly different—Woody had a kind of pigeon-toed stance—but that didn't help anyone to identify the brothers when they were standing still.

"Tell him who you are," our manager barked at Woody.

"I'm me," Woody said.

"Tell him your name and show them the number of your uniform."

"I'm Woody Strode and I'm number 18."

The ump looked at Corbett as if to say, What more do you want from me?

"I'm supposed to believe that bunch of malarky?" the Tigers' manager asked. "First of all, they changed numbers. Second of all, I know the difference between them two by the way they take their batting stance. Woody stands as if he's got a cake of ice up his rear." Corbett did a pretty good imitation of Woody at the bat, but Woody didn't like it none. There were times when I was glad that I was not the manager. "When I saw Woody out there," Cobett continued, motioning toward second, "I knew something was fishy."

"I'm here," Woody said. "Not out there."

"And I'm Santa Claus and in the North Pole," Corbett retaliated.

"Are you accusing me of something illegal?" Spike said. I looked at our manager blustering about and I knew what was going through his mind. He too was beginning to wonder whether Woody and Barry did change places without telling anyone. Managing identical twins was almost as bad as having to catch for a two-headed pitcher.

The ump kept bending down and sweeping the plate. I guess I would have done the same thing in his place. By the time McGurk got through with it, I could see my face in it, almost. McGurk straightened up and scowled. "What do you want me to do?" he asked. "Their own mother can't tell them apart. How can I do better than their mother?"

Our fans were booing because they were restless, but Corbett had worked himself into a real lather and wouldn't let go. I was antsy because I wanted to get up to bat and get it over with. "That bum on second batted out of turn," Corbett insisted. "He's out, he's out, he's out."

"Three outs doth an inning make," Nero Callahan said, and I thought that was pretty funny for a first baseman.

"I'm Woody," Woody said. Woody's brother out at second base remained where he was and said nothing. All of the rest of us had gathered around the managers and the ump. I guess Barry figured that absence makes the heart grow fonder.

"Prove it," Corbett demanded, spitting forth a shower of tobacco juice. How he chewed that stuff and lived was beyond me.

Spike thrust a finger under Corbett's nose. "My players don't have to prove who they are. I don't ask you who you are, and we all know you're a horse's ass."

The ump thrust the two managers apart. "One of us has got a birthmark on our backside," Woody volunteered.

"Yeah? Which one?" McGurk asked.

"I only got one backside," Woody said.

"I doubt it," Corbett said.

"Who's got the birthmark," the ump asked, "you or your brother?"

"One of us," Woody said. "I don't know which one." Woody was just stupid or he didn't know nothing. I picked up three bats and kept swinging away.

"You want my players to strip in front of all these women and children?" Spike asked. "All right, boys, undress," he shouted.

"That will be enough," the Ump said. "The first one who undoes so much as a belt is out of the game. Now everybody back where you belong. Maybe next season we'll get everybody tattooed with their name and number across their forehead, but this season is this season. As far as I'm concerned the man on second is who he claims to be, and I'm who I claim to be, and you are who you claim to be. Now let's play ball."

"I'm playing under protest," Corbett said.

"You do that," McGurk said, brushing off home plate once again. There wasn't a single speck of dust to be swept from it. Homer McGee, the Tigers' star reliever, was warming up in the visitor's bullpen. Corbett was no chump. He had bought a lot of warm-up time for his reliever. I stepped into the batter's box and the fans applauded. They weren't applauding me. They were applauding the fact that the game was starting again. "Play ball!" McGurk shouted.

What with the winning run hugging third, I shortened up on my grip some. The

Tigers' infield was pulled all the way in to cut off the run at the plate, and I had a hunch that Rosenthal's arm was cold after all that arguing and harumphing. My hunch was wrong, because the first ball Rosenthal threw me had more smoke on it than the Chicago fire. I didn't even get all the way around, and the ump yelled "Steeriiiike!" you know like those umps do who have never pronounced a single syllable word in their whole lives without making more of it than it is. All the while, Truman "The Ape" Hirsch was trying to rattle me with some painless chatter, but I paid him no mind. I had more important things to do than tell him my life's story. Off the field, I kinda liked the guy, but right then I coulda killed him. Baseball's that kind of game.

Since all I needed to do was hit a long fly ball, on the second pitch I swung from my heels, but I only got a piece of it. It was a fair-to-middling curve. I took the next pitch, a slider, for a ball. The fourth pitch from Rosenthal's steam machine I hit, but I came up under it. It was a towering pop fly on the first base side, and Callahan pulled it in easy. I was out, and The Professor was still studying third base like he was going to take a final exam.

Our catcher, Boris, the Mad Russian, came up next, and Rosenthal refused to show him anything good, because the Tigers were setting up the double play. Boris drew a quick walk, a semi-intentional one, and then Corbett came out and called in Homer McGee for relief. Our fans, being pretty good sports and all, gave Rosenthal a nice hand as he left the field. He didn't want to go, but what choice has a guy got? McGee took his warm-ups. He was a superstitious guy and we could see his red rabbit's foot sticking out his back pocket. Charlie Malone, our first baseman, was batting eighth, and he dug himself in pretty good. The outfielders were playing as shallow as they dared, and the infield was pulled back for the double play. It sorta gave the players a piggy-back effect. I suppose it was all quite exciting, but it didn't seem like much fun at the time. Those of us on the bench were sitting still, listening to last night's dinner rumbling in our stomachs. McGee didn't throw as fast as Rosenthal, but he mixed up his pitches well. His style was to pray to God and to nibble at the corner of the plate. Malone fouled off two pitches. On the third pitch, McGee went to the outside corner and Charlie missed it by an urban mile. The Professor tippy-toed back to third with a hang-dog expression upon his face. The fans groaned, moaned, booed, and breathed. It was like a terrible sigh. Two outs. The bases loaded. I could hear Charlie cursing himself to Kingdom Come. Sometimes you wish you were up there yourself; other times you thank the Lord that He saw fit not to put you in the hot seat.

Spike often told us: *Keep the game close and I'll come up with something.* Sometimes he did. This time he came up with a ghost.

Russ Oberlin, who relieved in the sixth, was due up next, so a pinch-hitter seemed mandatory. Trouble was there were only a couple of guys left, and the most likely candidate, because he batted lefty, was Ernie Baltimore Fleers. Trouble was that Ernie didn't hit very well when there were men on base. Spike looked down the deserted bench, and motioned to Paul Highlander to start warming up.

Then he studied the roster. He made a scratch mark on the scorecard and went to talk to the umpire.

"Play ball," McGurk barked at us.

"What do you think we're playing?" Spike said.

"You had better get a batter out here in two seconds," McGurk said.

"I got a batter in there," Spike said. "Can't you see him?"

The ump looked at Spike as if Spike had lost his marbles.

"Oh yeah? Who is it?"

"I'm sending Cat Crosby to bat for Oberlin." Spike turned toward the empty batter's box. "Go to it, Cat." McGee stood on the pitcher's mound and scratched his head. Spike started back to the dugout.

"Come back here," McGurk commanded. "Are you trying to make a monkey out of me?"

"Truman there's the ape," Spike said.

"I don't see anybody in the batter's box," McGurk said.

"Crosby's lost a lot of weight since the car accident," Spike said.

"One more remark like that," McGurk barked, "and you're out of the game."

"What's the problem?" Spike asked, as politely as he could. "Cat Crosby's on my roster. He's perfectly eligible to go into the game as a pinch-hitter."

McGurk must have thought that Spike had lost his mind. Otherwise, he wouldn't have been so patient. Maybe the strain of the game was too much. "Cat's in the hospital," McGurk explained, as if he were talking to a potentially violent child. "I read it in the paper myself." The Tigers' manager had already joined the confab.

"What's going on?" Corbett asked. "McGee is ready to pitch." It looked to us that McGee was ready to explode. He was pacing back and forth like a tiger in heat.

"I'm just trying to get a batter up there so we can finish the game," McGurk said.

"I *got* a batter up," Spike said. "It's the other side that's delaying the game."

Corbett looked at McGurk. I guessed they both thought the same thing, that Spike was losing his grip. We were beginning to wonder ourselves. "He don't have to set up a batter if he don't want to," Corbett said hopefully. "My boy's ready to pitch."

"Cat Crosby is with us in spirit," Spike said. "I'm sending him up to bat."

"I don't care who you send up to bat," Corbett said, "as long as you don't pull another Woody and Barry switcheroo."

McGurk made up his mind. "All right," he said. "If that's what you want." McGurk pulled down his mask and took his position behind Truman "The Ape." Spike returned to our wondering faces and slumped down onto the bench. McGee circled the pitcher's mound, rubbing his rabbit's foot.

Fleers had selected his bat. "Are you going to send me in?" he asked.

"I got a batter up there," Spike said. "Can't you see him?"

"Oh yeah?" Fleers asked.

"Play ball!" the ump cried. Corbett ran out to the mound to calm his pitcher. McGee rubbed the rabbit's foot, scratched his head, then spat.

"What the hell is going on?" McGee wailed.

"Nothing," Corbett said. "Just pitch. They got nobody up there, so all you got to do is get the ball over the plate."

"What's this talk about Crosby's spirit?" McGee asked, wiping the sweat from his forehead.

"Go to it, Crosby!" Spike shouted. The manager turned to me. "Come on, Harry. Give the batter some encouragement."

I was straining so hard to hear what they were talking about out on the mound that Spike's suggestion took me a bit off guard. I looked around at the other players. Maury O'Neill shrugged. Charlie Malone held out his hands, palms up, as if to say our manager had lost his grip. But what could I do? I was in no position to lead a mutiny. I climbed to the top of the dugout steps and clapped my hands. "Come on, Cat! Get a hit! Get a walk, even!" I felt like a fool shouting to a non-existent batter, so I could guess what McGee might feel like being asked to pitch to one.

Spike kept up the hollering, and soon Boris and Malone joined in. We had quite a chorus going. Then everybody joined. McGee looked in our direction with an expression of abject fear. I guess that was understandable. He was a lot more superstitious than I was.

McGee and Corbett were arguing back and forth something fierce. It was pretty obvious that McGee had doubts about pitching to a ghost. Hans Holtzman, the Tigers' third baseman, had trotted over to the mound to try to calm McGee down. Years later, when Holtzman and I got together for some drinks, he filled me on the details.

Woody Strode came up and stood beside me. At least, I think it was Woody. "Come on, Cat!" he shouted. "Get the run in!"

McGurk was halfway out to the pitcher's mound. "Let's get started," he barked.

"Get those bums to stop yelling," McGee pleaded.

McGurk looked over at me. "You guys calm down or I'll clear the whole bench."

"Come on," Woody shouted. "We can yell encouragement to our batters." I gave Woody a dig in the side, because I could see that the ump was at his breaking point. I couldn't blame the guy neither.

McGee started to walk away. "I ain't pitching to no ghost," he said.

Corbett grabbed his pitcher by the belt of his pants and swung him around. As Holtzman later told me, Corbett looked at McGee and said, "How can it be a ghost? Crosby's in the hospital and alive. Just throw three strikes and you're out of the jam."

"How do I know Crosby ain't dead?" McGee asked, clutching his red rabbit's foot.

"I don't have time to call the hospital to find out," Corbett said. He punched a finger into McGee's chest. "If you don't get back on that mound and pitch, you are out of baseball forever." Well, McGee thought that over and went back to the mound, and picked up the rosin. I glanced over at the Professor still on third. He was positively wilting. Corbett left the field, and Holtzman took his position.

The fans of course were adding to the confusion, because a lot of them didn't understand what was happening, and there was no way to stop the game to explain it to them. The fans must have thought we were crazy, all of us Whips shouting at the top of our lungs at a batter nobody could see. I was wondering what Cat Crosby felt, what with him lying there in his hospital room, listening to the game on the radio and hearing that he had been sent up to pinch hit for Oberlin.

It had taken a bit of doing, but finally McGee coaxed himself back to the rubber. He wiped his mouth with his sleeve. When we saw that he was going to pitch, we began to have some doubt ourselves. All he had to do was get three pitches over the plate, and there was no batter in the way to stop him. Truman "The Ape" Hirsch flashed a sign. McGee checked the runners. I felt a chill go down my spine, then up it. I looked back toward Spike. He was still on the bench looking pretty grim. After what seemed like forever, McGee turned loose with the ball. The ball was heading toward home plate, but it was so high that it soared all the way over the heads of the catcher and the ump. McGee had uncorked the wildest pitch I had ever seen in the history of the game. There was no way that Truman "The Ape" was going to chase it down in time. McGee rushed in to cover home. It was, however, a futile gesture at best. The Professor rushed in with the winning run. Even Barry, if he indeed were truly Barry, made it across with a run that was not even needed.

Of course we went wild. And the fans went wild. We were stomping, yelling, shouting, slapping, kissing, whooping, hollering, dancing, leaping. I doubt that I had ever been happier in my life, not even counting my first kiss from Suzie Davis.

We had trounced the Tigers by a score of 4-2, and were the champs, not chumps, of the Carolina League. Needless to say, Spike was quite a hero, and got all kinds of write-up in the press. So did the spirit of Cat Crosby. Even the Rules Committee got into the act, and wrote a rule saying that if no one came up to bat then it was to be ruled an automatic out. No one had even considered that possibility before. We had changed everything.

As for Homer McGee, the last time I saw him he was trudging off the field with his red rabbit's foot sticking out of his back pocket. I never saw him again. He never did return to pitch in our league.

Of course, the following year was the war itself. I had heard a rumor about McGee joining the Marines. But for me, that '41 season was the sweetest that ever was. Williams hit .406; DiMaggio had his streak; and a ghost had won a league championship for us. We had even changed the rules of the game.

The rest of the years right afterwards weren't nearly so good.

Williams' Last Game

"I felt nothing," he said.
"No sentimentality? No gratitude? No sadness?"
"I said nothing," Ted said. "Nothing, nothing."

Yeah, well we knew it all along.
If he had struck out we would have cried,
If he had walked
We would have lynched the pitcher & maybe
The manager
& well maybe the whole town of Baltimore,

But we knew something was going to happen,
Because he hadn't done much all day,
Walked in the 1st because Steve Barber
Wasn't throwing him much
& you know, if it's only a 10th of an inch
Outside the zone
Williams
Ain't going to swing at it, just watch it.

Ride by & then him loping off to 1st.
He does more walking in Boston
Than the postmen, if you know what I mean.
So then again in the 3rd he flies out to
Jackie Brandt,
So there really isn't much to talk about

Until the 5th, what with the Sox trailing
3 to 2, but the Kid really gets hold of one,
& the horsehide is flying, climbing
& 10,000 of us are up on our feet until
Al Pilarcik
Grabs it at the 400 foot mark.

& so all of us sit back down
& it's damp & there's not much wind.
I'm telling you it's a pretty gray day.

Later the Kid says
"I don't think I could hit one any harder
Than that. The conditions weren't good."
But Gus Triandos,
The catcher, just squats back down
& the game goes on, all of us knowing
That something has to happen,
Because that's no ordinary ballplayer up there
& if you can't believe in that,
What can you believe in, huh?
Ed Hurley
Starts calling balls & strikes again
& so we wait & so then it happens
Just the way it's supposed to.
Williams is up, see, & you know
It's going to be his last time at bat in Boston,
Except Jack Fisher's
Pitching now & not Steve Barber,

& then it happens. It's a 1 and 1 count, see,
& Fisher lets go with a fast ball,
But he doesn't get it there low enough,
The way he wants it. He goes a little too high
& Williams
Unloads one. I mean he unloads it,

& 10,000 of us are on our feet,
Screaming like crazy
WE WANT WILLIAMS,
WE WANT WILLIAMS,
& he's circling those bases with his head down
& you know it's going to be the last time,
& his head is down & everybody's screaming,
I mean
Who in the hell cares about the score,

& then he's in the dugout
& we're screaming
WE WANT WILLIAMS,
WE WANT WILLIAMS,
But he's not going to come out for us
Until at the end of the inning

Huggins sends him out to left field
With Carrol Hardy
Tagging at his heels
& then Williams turns & runs back.
Later *The Sporting News* says
SPLINTER TIPS CAP
TO HUB FANS AFTER
FAREWELL HOMER,
But that wasn't the way it was.
What he did was
Hit a homer his last time up,
His 521st homer,

& then walk away, not nodding
Not cheering, not tipping his cap,
Just walking away
Like a man who's done a good job
The best he can & knows it.
Now maybe he wants to be alone
Or with his friends in a bar somewhere.
Anyway, hitting a homer your last time up,
That's the way to go, isn't it?

The Pitcher Unnecessarily Delays the Game

⚐

Pos	B	T	Age
Earthling	L	R	50

Dummy Hoy. What was his lifetime batting average? Wait, it'll come to me. I'm one of those statistic freaks. I learned to count by having my father point out to me batting averages and the uniform numbers of superstars. My old man once led the Texas League in strikeouts, but that was in another country before we moved onto the Senator's estate. The Senator is saddling his horse. A huge chestnut. A tough one to break. Split-fingered fast ball. A tough one to hit. My father used to be the Senator's chauffeur—some comedown, huh? Not the Senators' chauffeur, which would have been more in keeping with our interests.

Dummy Hoy when did he play in the Majors how many other deaf players have made it to big-time baseball I suppose I could drag my weary carcass over to *The Baseball Encyclopedia* when Delia comes in. She's my once-a-week helpmeet, secretary, coffee-maker, letter-sorter I should pay her more but the sports articles aren't moving the way they used to with many of the old markets drying up *Baseball Digest* has sent back your piece on Pafko she says we just stuff it into another envelope keep them moving idiots **POINT OF REFER-ENCE:** I am ten years old or so and am riding a pretty ugly broken down horse. My father in order to get the nag to gallop runs ahead Hang on tight Marie and down I go my old man running on foot to some wasteland he starts to gallop the horse I mean I am frightened because the horse is running too fast for me who was the fastest player to run from home to first Mantle was pretty fast when he had his legs legs are not easy to come by I want a woman with legs Delia has legs I enjoy looking at her legs I keep looking high up as high up as she will allow which is not always too much the DiMaggio brothers banged out 4,853 hits among them with Joe, of course, having the majority of them and I really should give old Vince a call and find out how's he feeling how it feels to be in the shadow of two more skilled and beloved brothers but maybe his mother loved him the most mothers being what they are what are they and I can't hold on much longer I can't hold on I topple from the saddle Delia gives me another stack of questions for my column but I just don't have the energy to look up the answers.

POINT OF REFERENCE: If you can look up the answer, is the question worth asking?

I topple from the saddle and fall into the loose gravel I am crying what's the matter Delia asks you really feeling the blues today got more official rules on balks by pitchers quicksand self pity my father of course is worried about me but he is also worried about the horse it has run off to a fetid canal behind the gas station or suppose it slips off the side of the mountain and disappears forever will he have to reimburse the Senator for the loss of course he will. The Senator counts every nickel where will he get the money even I begin to worry about the horse and hate myself for falling off Delia I need another mount been my secretary for nearly a dozen years now and never have been to bed together just to reduce the sexual tension between us should have gotten a male secretary but who wants another man around you're ahead in your columns she says you can afford to take a few days off No I can't get back on I can't you got to my old man says and the white horse comes out of the shadows and patiently asks if you could just have one book on a desert island which one would it be *The Baseball Encyclopedia* of course the most important book ever published more important than the Bible crops grass as if nothing has happened on grass? No Delia says she stays off that stuff she's 36 and living with some dumb jock who doesn't appreciate her I'm fifty and over the hill and divorced fans send in questions the Dummy Hoy questions are a good example. From people too lazy to do a little research on their own or who are too poor to own a few basic reference books what was wrong with the Pafko article doesn't anybody say no they just send it back as if you have no feelings no rent to pay more postage wasted and so while my father is cajoling me to return to my life as a cowboy star the Senator is riding his huge chestnut and he is playing around for reasons that will never fully be explained why Delia and I aren't sleeping together making whoopee in the middle of the afternoon letting life pass us by the Senator forces his hand inside the mouth of the horse section 8:05 of the Book of Life states "If there is a runner or runners . . ." and the horse bites, a great gash in the back of the Senator's sunburnt freckled hairy hand. Bleeding profusely. What major leaguer bled more than all the others? Oh Tris Speaker, where are you when I need you?

The Senator's mistress, who is riding by his side, hands him a handkerchief to tie around his wound eli eli (A) the rider, while touching his mount makes any motion naturally associated with his pitch and fails to make such delivery from where I am standing, in khaki pants torn by the pebbles, glass, stones, humiliations endless your story on Maglie has come back if live long enough everything comes back hah! Let's go shopping Delia says that's her answer to everything. We have time before the game. When the weather's nice. I often take Delia to the games. It's better than giving her a raise.

I'm burning out I tell her. I am like the final human comet chasing my own tail through the entopic universe. Abbott and Costello. One night in the Entropics. My father, hearing the Senator swear, is embarrassed. Embarrassed for me if he could only hear me now spreading her legs what man came to bat most in the single season but the Senator dismounts walks to the front of his horse. He forces the mouth to open. He grabs the horse's tongue and pulls it out. Rabbit Maranville I say. You're right says Delia who is checking up on me. My father puts me back onto Yankee Knight the name of my trusty steed and this time the horse does not run. I have a gentle walk, a trot toward the barn. It is important if you fall off your mount that you get right back on Sex it all comes to sex Slide Kelly.

Jimmie Foxx 534 home runs. Hank Aaron 755 home runs. Yankee Stadium. Zero home runs. Do you ever think of doing something else? Yankee Stadium can't do anything else. The radio is playing Where Have you Gone Joe DiMaggio? What am I doing? Putting your hands where they don't belong Delia says. The antique store on the way to the game is no bigger than a horse's tongue. The original price for a black locket is eighteen dollars, but today it is on sale. Half price. Ladies' Day at the Ballpark. She thinks quite awhile before buying it I study her figure not bad and her long blonde hair and her long legs I should really give her a raise eventually there are going to be no markets at all I feel like a heel. She removes ten dollars from her red pocketbook and places it on the glass counter, running her hand over the bill to get the wrinkles out.

Methodical. That's what she is. That's why I hired her. Pct. 969. Fielding. Tom Jones. That old chestnut: No run, no hit, no Fielding. Really I should have bought it for her. Then every time she wears it she will think of me. I want someone to think of me who doesn't Pafko. It's not that bad a piece will do on a rainy day she will What are you going to do with it I ask the woman who runs the store excuses herself because the phone is ringing associated with his pitch and fails to make such a delivery. The owner of the antique store is about the same age, build, height as Delia. When she picks up the phone I notice that the woman's hands are covered with scratches bruises red varnish she notices my noticing a threesome a hotel with mirrors on the ceiling?

"I'll wrap the locket myself and pretend I've gotten it from a secret admirer," Delia says. "That'll make John jealous." John is the man she's living with. Another ex-baseball player. A first baseman qua slugger with only three seasons in the minors before . . . well, before. His right eye is covered with a patch.

"You can tell him it came from me," I told her.

"That won't make him jealous."

"You know how to hurt a man." I smile but it hurts. No man wants to be thought of as being harmless. We regret that we cannot use at this time your . . . I make Delia open the locket again. I am always attracted to empty lockets. They suggest so many possibilities.

I can hear the owner of the antiques on the phone. I make no pretense of not paying attention. (B) the lover, while touching her body, fails to step directly toward the mound "No, he's a good boy," she's saying, possibly a lawyer. "Just a little hot-tempered."

"I'll give you my picture to put inside it." John had been playing with dynamite caps he was working with when one went off unexpectedly He's a good boy the woman on the phone repeats, "I mean he did discover them in bed together. The law has to take that into account."

The law. .321. "I'll put Whit's picture inside it," she says. "Not yours." Whit's her son. Delia's. I too have sons but we've lost track of one another. A book about fathers and sons who have played in the major leagues. Need some kind of advance. I could have purchased a copy of Phil Rizzuto's contract once. At one of those Sports Memorabilia Shows. It paid him all of $15,000 a year. Holy Cow!

"No, no, no," the woman says. "I've got money. I want him out. He's a good boy."

Who was that member of the Mets who was caught having sex with some woman other than his wife and the owners forced him to apologize in public. Baseball's long history of humiliating their players. One traded for a dozen dough-nuts.

The Pitcher unnecessarily delays the game. . . .

POINT OF REFERENCE: "I have been reading your column for many years now and enjoying it. Could you tell me how many players have been prac-ticing Druids?" Sometimes, when you come across tantalizing trivia you have to make up your own questions. Question and answer people do it all the time. Grantland Rice. Socrates. The one great scorer is marking against my name Delia and I are in the first row behind the catcher. Nothing between us and the action on hand but a mesh fence to keep spectators from being creamed in the kisser. Bob Turley is on the mound. He's fast but wild. It's early in the season, so there really isn't too much at stake yet except everybody knows that the Red Sox aren't going anywhere not even when everybody in their line-up is batting over .300. Pitching is the name of the game. The chestnut horse had to be shot to be put out of its misery. Why doesn't someone shoot the Red Sox and put them out of their misery.

Delia puts her arm every finger over mine. Would John shoot us if he caught us in bed together. Strike three. You're out! With the beer buzzing and the sun shining and the temperature comfortable I'm beginning to think I'm going to have a chance with her my tongue inside her mouth her tongue inside my mouth and what kind of an idiot was that Senator anyway always trying to bring base-ball under the Interstate Commerce Commission which of course would make baseball liable for anti-trust actions. Want to start your own third major league? Go ahead. Just try it. This is the land of opportunity. The Home of the Braves. Across the street people in tenements are hanging out of windows, applauding. In spite of the fact that the Red Sox had managed to get the bases loaded, the police and the firemen without Virgil Trucks were trying to evacuate the stands. Indeed it is somebody's fire bombing, some madman or some religious sect de-voted to the hatred of horses and baseball and free love. I wouldn't put it past the Senator who must be behind it all who could reach into the mouth of a spirited animal and pull the tongue out how much I wanted Delia's tongue in my mouth it was not the fire nor smoke driving me crazy it was that thought of Delia's tongue and mound and the sirens going on and off, off and on, and the fire engines burning through the streets with sermons. Not just the bleacher on fire but the reserved seats as well and the boxes. This is the House That Ruth Built. This is the Bomb that lay in the house that Ruth built to call time and the players are concentrating intently with Billy Martin wiping the sweat from his face and

Vern Stephens and Dom the brother of Joe still at their game because even if the world should end baseball is the most perfect thing that man has ever invented and there are many of them who would experience no sadness whatsoever if we were burned alive. People in the tenements around the Stadium were hanging out of windows, applauding was Delia's husband among them, holding binoculars to his eye, a waste of a good binoculars, a telescope should be plenty good for a one-eyed man and Dear Mr. Christian: Could you please in your Pilgrim's Progress send me some And the sirens. On and Off. On and Off. Not unlike the system used to program computers, and the fans cheering and many of them booing Tris Speaker was my childhood hero and it was not until I was a grown man with children of my own that I learned that my own father disliked my hero because at one point, my father had tried to get me an autographed baseball and the center fielder had refused to sign any autographs for us and my old man had never really forgiven my hero for that but there were really no heroes anymore certainly not heroes in the Arthurian tradition what with liable for anti-trust suits and What-not information about Pete Gray, the one-armed outfielder of course baseball is not the whole cosmos. In the aisles so many of the fans are galloping over one another shouting themselves hoarse pushing pulling screaming lunging falling screeching burning that I pull Delia over the railing that separates the spectators from the playing area. Sammy White is coming to the plate and Delia almost bumps into him but he is so intent upon singling the winning home run that he pays us no mind. We're running toward the bullpen area. "The Locket!" Delia remembers. "I've dropped my locket."

"We're not going back for it now," I tell her. "You can't find it anyway. Not with all those people." Over 40,000 persons, all on fire. The smell of fried flesh is overwhelming.

"I've got to find it!" The concession stands are crumbling. Falling. All that beer foaming. A river of boiling head. This is the malt that lay in the house that Ruth built. No Achilles to leap in to stem the tide. 3 to 3 in the top of the fifth. On the field the temperature has reached over 100 degrees. Rizzuto's uniform is sticking to him, dripping. The metal on the catcher's mask is so hot that Yogi can't bear to touch it, can't take it off without peeling away his face.

"But there's nothing in it." I tug her harder. But she breaks free. I run ahead, hoping she will follow, but she doesn't. She simply stands stone still, tears streaming down her face. Four or five children, their clothing ablaze, fall from the upper deck onto the wire fence in back of the catcher, not far from where Delia and I had been sitting. They are like tiny rockets.

"I have it," I call to her, holding out my fist.

"You have it?"

The players, however, refuse to move. The Boston catcher takes the first two pitches and fouls one off. He's no Yogi Berra, but he's all right.

"I found it," I lie. I am perfect at lying even in Hell. When she approaches to take the locket, I put my arms around her and she presses her face into my shoulder and I carry her off the field. The scoreboard is filled with zeros. Zero that most wonderful of all creations after baseball.

There is an Art Museum up the street where many of the wounded are being carried. The street is filled with the dead and dying, parts of human bodies in the gutter, all manner of fluid flowing into the sewers. The sirens refuse to stop wailing. What will Casey say when he is finally called before the Senate Subcommittee on Antitrust and Monopoly? *"Now the second thing about baseball that I think is very interesting to the public or to all of us is that it is the owner's fault if he does not improve his club, along with the officials in the ball club and the players.*

"Now what causes that?"

What does cause it? Radios of all shapes and sizes are going full blast every citizen of the Big Apple trying to get the news of the fire bombing. Are the fans getting out of hand? Too much violence in sports? *"Of course, we have some bad weather. I would say that they are mad at us in Chicago, we fill parks."*

The Senator has gone on the air to reassure the public that it's not the end of the world. We're told not to panic. Holy Cow!

T	Wounded	Dead	IP	Total Base Runners
Bombs	34,965	7,118	5	42,073

Cops are dragging the wounded and bleeding over the glass cases of the mummies bodies are piling up in the hallways Delia's blouse is ripped and her skirt is covered with dirt the locket is far from her mind and her face on my shoulder reminds me of Yankee Knight of so long ago. I run my hand through her hair, her hair, her hair. We are both out of breath and wondering dazed breathing.

Through the windows of the museum we can see Yankee Stadium burning and the blaring sirens and the fire engines blazing through the burning streets give me a headache the kind of headache I often received as a young child and I turn to watch Delia running from patient to patient doing what she can to bring comfort help aid, doing what she can to stem the tide of disaster. I look at Delia's pear-shaped breasts as she bends over a white-haired man crying out for his lost grandchild. Hey, old man, can you tell me the names of the only two players to compete in major league games in four different decades? Does John worry about her. Does he know we have gone to the game? Or does he think we have snuck off to a hotel? "He's a good boy," the old man says, and Delia takes his hand as if she is holding an antique something tender and fragile from another era like baseball itself. (C) The pitcher delivers the ball to the batter while not facing the batter.

Downstairs, the police are trying to barricade the front doors. Too many people have been admitted to the make-shift emergency room. The museum cannot hold us all. "Move downstairs," one of the Museum Officials pleads to us. "We can't hold this much weight. The floor is beginning to buckle."

The weight of the dead and dying is too much to bear. It's a good thing that so many of us are missing.

"What did he say?" the old man asks Delia.

"He said: 'What was the need for this legislation?' I wonder if you would accept his definition. He said they didn't want to be subjected to the *ipse dixit* of federal government because they would throw a lot of damage suits on the *ad damnum* clause. He said, in the first place, the Toolson case was *sui generis,* it was *de minimus non curat lex.*"

"Oh."

I have a shoe box at home filled with old baseball cards and some of them give you the exact weight and height of the baseball player that is pictured, but Delia refuses to give up. She is tearing her own clothing to make bandages and I am falling deeper into love or lust from which I cannot work my way out or back. The Museum Officials refuse to allow the unwinding of the mummies, but of course nobody listens. I am soon unravelling history with a capital H and mummy cloth is being put to work winding around breasts and brows and legs and chests and the floor is collapsing the stairs go first there must be over 500 people on the wooden staircase with its fancy balustrade the banisters the survivors from the fire falling falling to the marble floor heads bashed open brains spilling staircase with its fancy balustrade the banisters the survivors from the fire falling falling to the marble staircase with its fancy balustrade the banisters the survivors falling falling to the marble and then the second floor crowd panicking feeling the floor moving away from them until nearly a hundred of us are pushed through the plate glass window and I am falling through the air shouting Delia Delia Delia and I think the pitcher, while touching the plate, accidentally drops the ball. And Dummy Hoy? What about him, you ask. Actually his real name was William Ellsworth Hoy, but he was called "Dummy" because he was deaf and dumb.

	Games	At Bats	Hits	Home Runs	Batting Average
Hoy	1798	7123	2054	40	.288

I call and call and call, burning in love, but no one hears. Hoy! Hoy! Ahoy! But baseball is not the whole world.

Baseball is not the whole world.

Mike Schmidt Announces His Retirement

"I've no idea where Schmidt will rank in twenty
years, but at this time he is clearly the greatest."
—Bill James

I suppose one cd. say how difficult it is to hit 548 homers,
But how much more difficult it must be to say good-bye to one's own life:
"I left Dayton, Ohio, with two bad knees
And a dream of becoming a baseball player.
I thank God it came true."
The wits say dreams that come true hurt the worst of all,
That answered prayers are a curse,
But baseball is not a game of wit,
It is a game of grace,
Of watching something disappear, gracefully,
Tho sometimes we cannot hold back the flood of emotion.
2 hits in his last 41 at-bats:
"I feel I could ask the Phillies to keep me on to add to my statistics,
But my love of the game won't let me do that."
The strong man cries.
He chokes up. The words won't come.
17 seasons of dispensing grace to believers and non-believers alike,
17 seasons and now in the locker room it's Loonie Tunes:
"That's all folks!"
With Reggie Jackson & his candy bar a bit higher on the list,
And Mickey Mantle a little bit below.
No wits in lists. 8,352 at bats.
"It's the friendships I have made that I will cherish the most."
And the silence. The arc of a ball so small you can hold it in your hands.
No words in a home run. Going going gone.

Johnny Inkslinger,
at the Baseball Hall of Fame,
Pays Homage to Babe Ruth

Blaise Pascal wrote: "Man is but a reed—
The weakest thing in nature...."
But he had not seen Ruth in action.
Obviously another blind Homer is needed
To do justice to the body politic of grand slam,
Horsehide sailing into aurora borealis.
The Great Bambino answering hermaphroditic critics
By giving them the finger,
The summer of 89: Prince is doing his Batdance,
While in our hearts The Sultan of Swat,
Larger than auld lang syne
Bowlegs the bases, his head down,
Tipping his cap to Roland Barthes,
Muttering under his beerstained breath
"Hundes, wollt ihr ewig leben?"
The brabble of the crowd must be nothing to him &
Everything. How quickly they turn on you,
Seams unravelling in the vapor lock of love.
When someone points out that George Herman Ruth
Earns more money than the President,
He says matter-of-factly,
"I'm having a better year than he is."

Why Baseball's Hall of Fame Passed Me by This Year

It was the Key Largo Tigers
Against my Hollywood Cubs,
With my team in 1st
Tied with two other clubs,

But little could I know
As I oiled my mitts,
That I should walk to the mound
To give up 42 hits.

The 1st Tiger tripled;
I merely shrugged.
The next batter homered;
Into home they both chugged.

Gomez, Hardy, Swenson, Cross, Megs,
Hargin, Tobey, Ollie, & Willy:
Those Tigers troop through my dreams
Like tanks through jelly.

To make a long story short,
At the end of the 1st,
It was 16 to nothing,
But my team had seen worse,

For I was the solitary pitcher
That my club possessed,
So onward I plugged
Merely vaguely distressed.

Gomez, Hardy, Swenson, Cross, Megs,
Hargin, Tobey, Ollie, & Willy,
By the end of the game
Had run themselves silly,

But from my loyal teammates
There was barely a squawk;
I had given up 42 hits
But nary a walk.

My outfield had soared
Like a trio of gulls;
My infield has scampered
Fielding like miracles.

As up to the plate,
Hargin, Ollie, etc. paraded,
I knew in my heart
That I soon would be traded,

But no, but no,
This saga's not done,
Until I tell you the score:
Them 28, us 31.

When great wonders are listed
For your daughters & sons,
Kindly mention the day
I scattered 28 runs.

Trojan War Scorecard Discovered

After 150 years or so of excavation at the site of Ilium, archaeologists have finally unearthed solid proof that the Trojan War was an historical reality. A few months ago Dr. H. Schliemann of Brown University struck pay dirt when his shove touched upon an ancient scorecard. "The scorecard presents a shorthand retelling of all the events that Homer so wordily presents in his epics," Dr. Schliemann said. "In fact, there is a good possibility that Homer himself had access to this document when reciting his poem. He may well have used it as a trot or pony to jog his memory." The scorecard will be sent to Cooperstown and will be one of the permanent exhibits there.

GREEKS	1	2	3	4	5	6	7	8	9	10	11	12	AB	R	H	RBI	E
Achilles																	
Agamemnon																	
Ajax																	
Odysseus																	
Calchas (DH)																	
Phoenix																	
Nestor																	
Castor																	
Diomedes																	
Menelaus																	
Totals																	

GODS	IP	H	R	ER	BB	SO	GODDESSES	IP	H	R	ER	BB	SO
Zeus							Hera						
Ares							Athena						
Hades							Aphrodite						
Hermes							Artemis						
Poseidon							Thetis						

TROJANS	1	2	3	4	5	6	7	8	9	10	11	12	AB	R	H	RBI	E
Aeneas																	
Antenor																	
Dolon																	
Hector (DH)																	
Paris																	
Priam																	
Sarpedon																	
Pandarus																	
Glaucus																	
															DESTROYED		
Totals																	

How To Read the Symbols:

(Each warrior is identified by a number on his shield.)

- = tossed spear
- = fought with a god
- = grounded into a force play
- = reproved a fellow warrior amidst battle
- = covered head to foot with blood & flies
- = withdrew under pressure from Achaeans
- = withdrew under pressure from Trojans
- = made a bad cast with his javelin
- = took a third called wound
- = popped out to Ares (god of war)
- = saved the fleet from flames
- = torched a ship

- = intentional walk
- = hit an enemy in the shoulder
- = groaned
- = attempted to elude destiny
- = disguised self as a mortal
- = dashed in among the rabble
- = spectacular performance facing death
- = slaughtered 2 warriors with single arrow
- = fell on the enemy
- = stole a base and/or a sacred statue
- = looted
- = triple play (applicable only to the Fates)
- = fell back out of rage

Casey At the Bank

The outlook wasn't brilliant for him earning much more dough,
The budgets had been blasted with more contracts left to go,
And with Barry Bonds rebuffed and all the owners crying doom,
A sickly silence fell upon the lawyers in the room.

The accountants tallied figures, while that file and rank
Clung to Eternal Hope which springs from every bank,
But Clemens preceded Casey, as did Conseco (José)
And the former was a lulu, and the latter acted lousy.

Clemens claimed 5 mil. and a brand new spending spree,
While Rickey, out in Oakland, cried "Renegotiate for me!"
But upon the owner's ledgers, grim economics sat, ·
So there seemed but little chance of Casey sharing in the fat.

There rose a lusty protest at evening time, diurnal,
It rumbled thru the columns of the trusty *Wall Street Journal,*
Seconded by sportswriters, repeated by their brothers,
For Casey, Strikeout Casey, wanted more than all the others.

Across baseball diamonds, there went up a muffled roar,
Like the collapse of Savings Bank upon New England Shores:
"Twenty million per season, with bonuses galore!"
But, Casey, Mighty Casey, shrugged, "I was hoping for much more."

"Greed," cried frightened fans, while others shouted "Fraud,"
But one scornful look from Casey and management was awed,
And saw Casey's agents with faces stern like Juno,
Demanding that their Casey be made number *uno.*

While lawyers wade thru contracts from Networks and from Cable,
Casey pounds with violence his fist upon the table
And now the owners holds out a contract, and now he lets it go,
And then the air is shattered with the force of Casey's "No!"

Oh somewhere in this land, Johnny cannot write,
Teachers overburdened, libraries shut up tight,
The homeless sleep upon the streets of our mighty nation,
But there's some joy in Mudville—Casey's gone to arbitration.

Ted Williams Storms the Gates of Heaven

☞

So much of life is waste. Pure waste. You send out stories, and the editors send them back. You send out poems, and the editors send them back. You send out essays, and the editors send them back. Where does all that wasted energy lead? Merely to an expanded and slothful postal service.

Libraries, of course, are mines of wasted energies, of men and women who have labored long and hard to produce materials nobody reads. Thus, whenever I go to a library I feel overwhelmed by loss. I track down and check out, if possible, those books and pamphlets that nobody has read. Salvage operations. Yes, call them salvage operations.

For example: in 1879 some nobody, because in America if you are not world famous, you are nobody, some nobody bearing toward oblivion the name T.S. Arthur, and not, alas!, T.S. Eliot (just the other day I noticed that the *Village Voice* spelled it T.S. Elliot—let that be a lesson to all students of immortality) wrote a book, yes for want of a better term let's call it a book, not relegate his unadorned prose to the lower level of pamphlets and ephemera, entitled *The Strike at Tivoli and What Came of It*. Published in Philadelphia by some long gone company named Garrigue, Mr. Arthur's book starts out to be about labor/management, for want of a better term let's call it relationship, but ends up to be just another sordid tract against the evils of drunkenness.

"They couldn't beat the spread," the black man at the bar had told me before I came to the park. "I told you they couldn't beat the spread. And none of you cowards wanted to bet with me."

You start in one direction and you end up in the other. You start a project and the project never gets finished. It gets lost or abandoned. There may be a planet where all the false starts, all the wasted efforts pile up like a mountain without name.

"Why are you telling me this?" Ted Williams asks.

Hiroshima Mon Amour. Approximately twenty years ago, I started an essay upon the great movie. I was a true film scholar at the time.

"Why are you telling me this?" Ted Williams asks.

SUPERINTENDENT (MR. THORNE)
If you men do not go back to work within the week, the owners of the mill are going to bring in hands from a distance and throw out all the strikers.

I even tracked down the film script. Read everything I could about the film. Studied it as best I could in a time long before video recorders made film analysis so accessible, so possible, so triumphantly minute.

"Why are you telling me all this??????????????????" Ted Williams asks, getting more impatient with me all the time. And who can blame him? He's almost eighty years old and he's come out of retirement to lead another left-handed assault against the record books. Of course, anything an eighty-year-old man does on the baseball field is going to be a record.

He's eighty years old but he's still everything he was. The rage inside him is pure. The Splendid Splinter. The Kid. The man who once spat at sports reporters, criticized draft boards, gave up five of the most splendid seasons of his career to serve his country in the marines. And today his sympathies go out not to the belly-achers and academic air-heads, blow-hards who retreat behind columns of rhetoric to defend their exploitation of fellow creatures less fortunate than themselves, treating their part-time colleagues with absolute contempt, or, even worse, complete indifference, part-time instructors exploited through the teeth, while the tenured and sinecured great minds roam the corridors humming the tunes of sabbatical. But Ted is right. Why am I telling him all this? Today his sympathies are with the poor down-and-out Irish fighting for their jobs. Real people with real problems.

SUPERINTENDENT
Take my advice and keep yourself and your friends out of the clutches of the law. No one questions your right to lay down our work, if you are not satisfied with the wages paid. But if other men can be found who are ready and willing to take up your work as you are laying it down, they must be left free to come into the places you have been foolish enough to abandon. So I give you fair warning. The Corporation doesn't intend to wait much longer, and it doesn't mean to advance the rate of wages.

"Did you decide to return to baseball because of the money, Ted?"

Williams shakes his head. The way he talks, the way he stands, the absolute authority that he emanates—it makes you think of John Wayne, how John Wayne should have played the lead in *The Ted Williams Story*. And probably now it never will be made because the time has passed for those kinds of films. The age of heroism is dead. Long gone. And I wonder if that perhaps is not the real reason why the Kid, even at eighty we dare not call him anything else, bears with him, in his legends and towering home runs, something that is ageless and priceless.

"Couldn't beat the spread. All they did in the fourth quarter," the man at the bar told me, "was blitz, blitz, blitz."

Of course, coming out of retirement at age eighty has thrown the Hall Of Fame people into a tizzie. You have to be inactive to be in Baseball's Hall Of Fame. Your career has to be all over. Finuto. Caput. Ted's return to Boston has caused the rules committee to rupture a duck.

ANDY
Two sides will have to say to that, Mr. Thorne. And I give you fair warning,

Mr. Superintendent, that we're none of us going to submit to any interference in this business. It's our strike; and it'll be a sorry day for him as dares come in between us and our rights—it will!

"Was it the money?"

Ted shakes his head, pulls a cap from his back pocket, picks up one of his customized Louisville Sluggers. "It's not the money. The owners can give their players $50,000,000 a year and it wouldn't make a difference to me. If Musial and myself and DiMaggio had played in the hey-day of the super-contract, they could never pay us what we would be worth. There's got to be satisfaction in that, in knowing that nobody can ever pay you what you're worth."

I guess he's right about that, but I have never been in that position.

"What's Bertrand Russell getting?"

"What's he batting?" Ted asks. With him that's the essential question. Not the religion. Not the philosophic stance. Not the color of skin. Not the status in society. Not the weekly payroll check. Just simply and forever: "What's his average? How many home runs? How many runs batted in?"

"Nothing. He can't hit."

"Couldn't beat the spread, and nobody had the guts to bet with me," the black man had said.

Ted shakes his head. "What's money to me? Didn't I always have enough? Didn't my family? My family never wanted for things."

"After the '46 World Series, didn't you give your whole share away to Johnny Orlando, the clubhouse boy? Didn't you?

"That's me. Saint Francis Assisi of Fenway Park." He runs, jogs rather, to take his place in left field. An eighty-year-old man with the sun falling on his shoulders, his white hair gleaming in the sun. The pigeons and the larks and the nightingales and the vultures—everything with feathers and fur—gather about him while he tosses them bread and cracker crumbs. Fox and possum and bear run from beneath the bleachers. Ted pulls his cap to his head as if to say to the empty stands, to the world at large, "Take that, you bastards! The Kid is back and what are you going to do about it?"

The committee has already done something about it. The plaque honoring the Kid has been temporarily removed from the wall. A gray canvas covers the larger than life statue of Number 9 swinging from his heels.

The Kid's alive but the statues and trinkets are dead.

SUPERINTENDENT (MR. THORNE)

There's no reason in arguing the matter, Andy, nor in losing your temper over it. So far as the corporation is concerned, the question is settled. In three weeks from today, the engines will be fired up, the machinery set into motion. The mills will have their full complement of hands. Whether you or your friends in this useless strike shall be found among them or not will depend on yourselves. And now, gentlemen, I want to say a word to you about this striking business. There is no denying the fact that, somehow, things have gone wrong with you, and that you are getting worse and worse off every year, instead of better. How are you going to keep bodies and souls together much longer, unless some change takes place, is more than I can tell.

COMMITTEE MEMBER

We can't, sir, on the present wages, Mr. Thorne, and that's just why we're on strike. It's the wages, sir. That's what's the matter.

It's as if the men of Tivoli are speaking directly to Ted. It's not only his eyesight that is so extraordinary, even at his advanced age (it was said he could count the stitches on a ball in flight or number the angels on the head of a pin, the scales on a salmon from one of his Canadian rivers, the miles of the rivers themselves, and the droplets, dig, tug, and thickness of moonlight upon a forest carpet, the wattage of floodlights balanced precariously beyond the green monster), but also his hearing that allows him to hear the most minute throbbings of the heart.

"Why are you saying all these things about me?" Ted asks, suddenly overwhelmed and ashamed, like a man who has had just so much good luck thrust into his hands and then becomes forever afraid to open them for fear the luck will fall through, drain away, leach toward the lines that demark foul from fair. What you do in that case is form a fist and batter the gods into submission or take up a bat and swing with so much grace that it becomes not a matter of mechanical motion, but something far beyond anatomy, something of the natural, like the fall of rain or a slight turning of wind or a shadow.

"What about the changes in the strike zone?" I ask him.

"There's only one strike zone in baseball now," he says now, laughing, because there is no one in the stands to boo him, no die-hard blow-hard to rub the magic from the game because of envy or fear; "it's from early April to the middle of June. Usually by then the strike is settled." He roars. His own jokes please him, just as his own singles, doubles, triples, and home runs soothe him.

But the strike at the Tivoli Mills is not so easily settled. Nor anything of the past. We think of History as events that have been settled, but of course they never are. Someone is always coming out of retirement to knock over the apple cart.

SUPERINTENDENT THORNE

Gentlemen, I understand you. I don't blame you for striking. I don't see how you can help it, or how anything else can save you from ruin and starvation. The only wonder to me is that you didn't strike long ago.

ANDY

What do you mean by this, Mr. Thorne . . . is it trifling with us, you are?

"You talk about waste," Ted says, "but think of the year I hit .400, the last major leaguer ever to do it. What does it mean? It means for every ten times I went to bat, there were six times I came up with nothing, came up empty. Does that mean those six times at bat were useless? I should say not," Ted says, turning his head to look out at the landscape, the broken glass, the homeless, the vultures feeding on carcasses of dead lions. We are on the way to Tivoli. Not the Garden of Tivoli, that old pleasure garden, but to the mills where the men and women and children are starving. Starving because all they want is a living wage, fair wages for fair work. Because all they want is not to be exploited, not to be trampled upon, not to be turned inside out by a system whose philosophy centers around one simple but intricate proposition: How did that money or property get into the other person's pocket in the first place? Implying, of course: Is that other person with property more deserving than I who have none?

"No," Ted continues. "Maybe when I struck out, I was learning something about the pitcher, what he threw in that particular situation. Maybe I was learning something about myself. How to wait and swing from, not the heels, but the hips. The secrets of hitting are in the hips and wrist. Hitting a baseball is one of the most difficult things a human being can do, and six out of ten, or seven out of ten, the attempt leads to failure. But wasted effort? One might as well claim that all the past is failure."

SUPERINTENDENT THORNE

This affair is altogether too serious for trifling. Striking is well enough in its way, and men ought to strike against wrong, oppression, and plunder. As I have said, I don't blame you for striking; but I do blame you for striking against your friends instead of your enemies; against those who are helping you to feed and clothe yourselves and your children, instead of against those who are wasting your substance, and sucking out your very life's blood.

"The truth is," I tell Ted, "that the aim of society is to make you have yourself. Once you have learned to blame yourself for every failure, once you have become riddled with self-loathing, then society takes you by the hand and says, 'Welcome, friend, now you are one of us.'"

"I never listen to sentences that begin 'the truth is,'" Ted says, as we scramble aboard the trolley car that will take us from Fenway Park, that beautiful bandbox, that icon of summer, that core of whatever is pastoral within us. I, with my arms laden with Louisville sluggers and boxes of baseballs, follow him up the narrow steps. Clang, clang, clang, go the bells of my heart.

All my youth I was Williams's greatest fan. I followed his every action, his every batting title, his every fall from grace, as if he were, as all childhood heroes must be, some extension of my secret wish. Go against the shift. If they put ten people between first and second, still knock the ball there with all your might, all your fury. Don't go the other way. God has constructed a Boudreau Shift as a test against all inferior souls. Self-destructive behavior? Perhaps. But there is no need to destroy one's self when there are so many strangers and friends out there ready, willing, and able to do it for you.

SUPERINTENDENT THORNE
Strike against the whiskey mills and you'll have no need to go any farther! The trouble lies there and not in your wages. If you were getting double what you receive, and didn't strike against the whiskey mills, you'd be no better off than you are today. Tom Maguire and Bill Maloney would only go dressing up their wives and daughters at your expense, while your own children go about in dirt and rags.

ANDY
You are insulting me and my friends and we won't stand to hear any more of your lies.

When the men at the Tivoli Mills see Ted Williams climb down from the trolley, a great cheer goes up from the crowd.

"You with us, Ted? You with us?"

The question is an insult, because the answer is obvious. Ted merely nods. The owners of the Mills peer through their top-floor windows and turn white.

"What's an eighty-year-old baseball player doing here?" one of the owners asks, taking out his pocket watch and playing loosely with the winding knob.

"What's he going to do? Spit at us?" The owners, all four of them overweight and paunch-bellied, and dressed in black suits, break out with fits of laughter. But their hands tremble as they reach for the water pitcher that stands like an island of ice atop the long mahogany table.

The wives of the striking men are not that impressed with the Splendid Splinter. After all, he is eighty years old. And he is alone. He has not brought anyone else along. Only me, the perfect factotum, the chronicler of his exploits and supplier of equipment. Perhaps I should have done more with my life, but the strikers at Tivoli and I share a terrible burden, knowing as we do that America is not exactly the land of opportunity for everyone. It is the land of illusion, the illusion of opportunity, a network of secret societies and Good Old Boy Clubs. Insider trading and all that. Good Old American Pie.

One of the women calls out to my brother-in-law Andy who is leading the strike. "I say, Andy Sullivan, we're starving, we are, and the babies are crying. You must give in."

Give in. Give in. The very words make my blood go cold. They are the words I have heard all my life. Play by the rules of the game, and don't waste time trying to fight city hall. Just what Oceanos, father of all those daughters just as fear is the father of story telling, told to Abner Doubleday when he stole fire from the gods.

"It's just a myth," Ted says, picking up his bat, feeling the exact weight of his life in his arms and wrists and hands.

"Prometheus," I say, wiping the sweat from my forehead and eyes. The

August heat is stifling. The women in their rags and the children in their nakedness walk around and around the red-brick buildings, the dust rising behind them
in the sunlight. A swirl of fire inside and out.

"Prometheus," Ted repeats, plucking a brand new, tightly wound cork-cored
baseball from the dozens or so I have carried, have lifted down from the fire-red
clanging trolley car as if they were jewels of great price. This is the far edge of
the world we have come to, where Might speaks first, and Violence is a *muta
persona*. "What did he hit?"

WOMAN #2

If we keep on much longer, there'll not be half a dozen men in the room
worth the powder it would take to shoot 'em. That's what we're getting from this
strike! It's only an excuse for our men to loaf and to laze about and to drink, with
our children crying until my heart almost breaks to hear them.

One of the strikers reaches out and grabs the woman by her birdlike wrists,
shoving her with unpremeditated fury backwards. "Shut up," he shouts red-faced
into the woman's red face. "Take yourself home, or I'll break every bone in your
body."

ANDY

You don't know what you're talking about, woman. We can't give in! We'll
just be trod under foot as if we were dogs. It's starving we've been, with the old
wages: and it's for life that we're a-struggling. Just see how it is with ye all; and
they living like kings with their broadcloth and silks and their satins, and their
feastings and carousings. I tell you we pay for it. We pay for it all with our sweat
and our very life's blood, and they grudging us every bit of crust, and turning
their noses up at us if we were scum and filth instead of men and women like
themselves, and just as good as they are. Give in! I'm ashamed of yez.

The Kid points to one of the third floor windows and all eyes follow. The
men stop arguing. Children stop weeping. The sun sizzles in the wind like a fire-
storm. With his right hand he tosses the ball into the air. The bat is resting slightly
off his shoulder.

WOMAN IN THE CROWD (KATE BARKER)

And I'm ashamed of you, Andy Sullivan, talkin' that sort of stuff among
starving women and children instead of going to work as ye might, to feed 'em.
The Corporation says, here's a dollar for you, and dollar and a half, or two dollars, according to the work; and ye say here's nothing, according to the loafing,
idling, and drinking.

TOM BARKER

Shut up, Kate.

MRS. BARKER

Go to work and feed your children, Tom Barker, but don't talk to me about shuttin' up! I won't go down. I never will believe in your striking.

And the Kid's bat whips through the air and everybody stops. The mouths of children hang open, eating more dust than they have eaten in their lifetimes. And the sound of the bat hitting the ball becomes a kind of timeless music, a clash of galaxies, and the ball leaves the bat with black dirt smeared over their faces as if they had crawled out of a mine somewhere, confronting the sunlight for the first time, lean ever so slightly backwards, their mouths too gaping, as the ball smashes through its target, one of the pristine panes of a third-floor window.

"Another one, kid," he says to me. And I fetch it as fast as I can, as if my entire life had been building up to this rage, rage for the poor, the hurt the maimed, the exploited, the neglected, the hungry, the homeless, the blind, the toothless, the ulcerated, the psychotic, the neurotic, the drunk, the sober. And another perfect arc and the bat meeting the ball, freeing one sphere from gravity, and the sound of glass splintering and the owners running for cover.

Even the women, tugging and pulling at their aprons, stop bickering and sense in the defeat of their men a slight moment of what everything could have been like if there had been only one slight splinter of justice in the universe.

Up, up, through the third windows, and the glass splintering. The Splendid Splinter. And the children, bare-legged, bare-footed, bellies rumbling, jumping up and down, applauding. No boos here. And the thunderclouds are gathering.

The Kid has worked himself into a fury. Every pitcher who ever struck him out, who ever tried to take a morsel of food from his mouth, every seen and unseen enemy. Karooooooooooooom! Barooooooooooooooom! Crash! Ball after ball. And then running out of baseballs, the children start fetching him stones and pebbles and boulders, until his Louisville slugger becomes pockmarked and dented. And his hands are blistering and bleeding. He's eighty years old for god's sake.

And now the thunderstorm is letting loose. But nobody breaks rank. Nobody runs for cover. Children still fetch stones. Women still wipe tears from their eyes. Men stand as if they had been stripped to nakedness, their eyes searching every broken window for salvation.

He turns to me. All the windows on the second and third floors have been smashed. Not one pane of glass intact. Now there are only the first floor windows to take care of. Simple line drives.

The police have arrived with their Paddy Wagons, but they too, handcuffs and billy clubs at belt, are frozen in their tracks. They feel helpless against the onslaught of History. Of Myth. Hollywood and Baseball. The only true myths America has ever had.

"You can't do that, Ted, I'm telling you," the police sergeant says apologetically.

"Who says?" Karoooooooooooom. A clean white stone leaves the bat and smashes yet another pane of glass. The men, women, and children have formed a circle around the batter, a living batter's circle, to protect their leader from further outrage. Would police interrupt Beethoven at his symphonies, Rembrandt at his portraits, Einstein at his equations? Something perfect needs perfect concentration.

"A hot dog," The Kid says. "I could use some hot dogs."

"How many?" I ask.

"I don't know. Two dozen. Three dozen. And some milkshakes. I'm hungry and I'm thirsty."

"Tired?"

"How can I be tired when I'm doing what I was meant to do with my life?"

"There's a lunch wagon two blocks down," Andy says. They're all ready to take my place, ready to go forth for stones or hot dogs or milkshakes or the gods and goddesses themselves.

But I assert myself and hot-foot it off in the general direction of the hot dog wagon, standing pure and white with striped awning on a side street. The police still have made no move to destroy the magic circle.

I guess they're waiting for reinforcements.

"Blitz, Blitz, Blitz. All afternoon," the man at the bar had said.

And the old Greek couple husbanding and wiving the hot dog wagon tear, burn, sizzle, mustard, and relish. Hurry, please, hurry.

I hear shooting and yelling at the factory grounds, but I decide to stay put. It's like most things in life: it is my affair and it isn't.

"You know the largest hot dog ever made in the United States," the Greek says, turning the dogs over on the grill, "was seventeen feet long, and five inches in diameter?"

"I'd like to get my hands on that," says a woman who stands next to me. She has red hair and a tight blue skirt, a white blouse. I recognize her as one of the Tivoli women, one of them working the crowd.

"Take your foul mouth somewhere else, Hillary," the Hot Dog man says. "Can't you see we're busy?"

"I really don't have time for a lecture on the history of hot dogs," I tell him. We're doing the best we can, son.

"Want a good time?" Hillary asks me. She reaches for a napkin to wipe a spot from her blouse, over her left nipple.

"I had a good time once," I tell her. "Once. A long time ago."

"Once is not enough." Sounds like someone is tossing bombs by the mills. So much waste. Oh hurry. Hurry.

My arms are loaded with hot dogs and milkshakes. I pay with money old and crumbled and dull. The change falls to the sidewalk, but I am too impatient to pick it up.

"Now there's a man in a hurry," Hillary says. She goes for the silver. The pennies she leaves in place.

Blitz. Blitz. Blitz.

"Harry M. Stevens discovered the hot dog, and Tad Dugan named them."

"Big deal."

The rain is coming down harder, making the hot dog buns soggy. And I'm only a block or two away from the white and awninged hot dog wagon when the rolls burst open and four or five of the hot-dogs fall to the street. I bend over to pick them up but, in doing so, I spill the chocolate milkshakes over my pants and shirt and tie and coat and shoes. This is not my day, I think, remembering the time the bat boy for the New York Yankees brought his idol Babe Ruth enough hot dogs to give the Great Bambino a stomachache heard around the world. The bat boy's name was William Bendix.

The Babe and The Kid. Is that a meeting of onomastic destiny? I step on a couple more hot dogs, then into a puddle. My shoes fill with water as do the cuffs of my pants. The napkins are so wet that they fall apart.

Frankfurters. Franks. Red Hots. Pups. Viennas. Wienies. Wieners. Here they are. In all their glory. Broken. Bruised. Dirty. Wet. Soggy. When I reach the mill, no one is there. The thunderstorm has driven everyone away.

Or the militia has.

The ground is littered with dead bodies. Andy Sullivan is face down in the mud. There's a hole through the back of his neck. His shirt is pressed to his body by the rain and blood. I put the remains of the hot dogs and chocolate shakes on the ground, and turn the body over. Poor Andy Sullivan. All he wanted was a fair shake in life. Frankfurters. Franks. Red Hots. Pups. Viennas. Wienies. Wieners. What is a baseball game without them? But Andy Sullivan has no use for them now.

I feel a hand tighten upon my shoulder. It's The Kid. I know it is. But I don't turn to look at him. I don't want him to see me crying.

"I've ruined the hot dogs," I tell him.

"It doesn't matter," he says. "They were ruined a long time ago."

"What happened?"

"The owners were pissed that I destroyed all their windows, and so they called out the National Guard to bring a halt to the strike."

"They can't do that."

"They've got the money. People with money can do anything they want."

"How come you didn't get hurt?" I turn to face him. He stands without a wound, a scratch. An eighty-year-old living wonder on the comeback trail. He has won the comeback of the year so many times.

"I kept hitting the bullets back as fast as they could shoot them. Besides they knew what would happen if they harmed me. It would spark a whole goddamn rebellion, a full-scale revolution. Besides I have a game to play tonight."

Together we walk back to the trolley.

"Why would you play tonight?"

He shakes his head.

All the while, I imagine him in another eternity, imagine him in heaven, standing in front of St. Peter's Gate. He holds a ball and a bat, and he tosses the ball into the air, and then he hammers it as hard as he can against the pearly gates. Smash. Smash. Smash. And the angels are singing "Hallelujah!" For the first time in the history of salvation, a mortal, though not a mere one, using spit and determination and all the skills at his command, fantastic hand-to-eye, eye-to-muscle coordination, is going to crash through the gates of heaven. Not even Christ is going to keep him out. Smash. And the ball sizzles into the golden lock. He's worked himself up into a fury and is smashing ball after ball into the giant gate. Gabriel and Michael and St. Peter try to interpose their nonsubstantial bodies between the line drives and the gate. Smash. Kaboooooooooooom! Hallelujah.

The milkshakes and hot dogs remain on the field of battle. "Such a waste," Ted says. "Everything is such a goddamn waste." It's a good thing he hadn't eaten them because he would have only gotten a fantastic stomachache.

"How can you play after all you've seen?" I ask him, but he doesn't answer. He senses the terrible waste inherent in words, in story-telling, in reaching toward the hearts of others. He stares straight ahead. Perhaps imagining the wide assortment of pitches that are going to be tossed him in the game that lies ahead.

The trolley car rumbles and the bells ring. Terrible Teddy. Teddy Ballgame.

I tell him my fantasy about him knocking down the gates of heaven with his line drives, but even as I speak, a pained expression clouds his face. "Why are you telling me all this?" he asks.

And the trolley car, newly painted, oblivious to the burdens it carries, turns toward Fenway Park with its thousands upon thousands of screaming and adoring fans.

"Why are you telling me all this?" he asks. "Why are you telling me all this?"

"You can't beat the spread," the man at the bar had said.

From **William Blake's** *Songs of Baseball*

Tigers

☞

Tigers! Tigers! Winning least
Near the basement of the East,
What mortal fans of baseball lore
Dare peruse today's box score?

Oh bring us deep & lasting mercy,
To inspire the pitching of J. Searcy!
Fleet be the feet of Robby deer
To give our fans a bit of cheer.

When your starts toss down their bats,
& your pitchers give up hits,
Does He smile His work to see?
Did He who made other teams make thee?

Tigers! Tigers! Burning least
Near the basement of the East,
What immortal eye or hand
Can ease the pain of Sparky Anderson?

You Know me, Bill—Ring Lardner's Sonnet

🏳

"If Ring Lardner ever wrote a sonnet, I've never
heard about it."

—Adolphe Menjou

That time of year thou mayest in me behold
When rookie hurlers, or some or few, do hang
A sliding curve which strikes against the cold
Bat of the hitter where late my fastball sang;
Girlie, in me thou see'st the twilight of such day,
As after the Giants fadeth in the west,
Which by and by a rummier bunch doth take away
Another pennant, that seals up all the rest.
Girlie, in me thou see'st the dimming of a career
That on the ashes of my pitching arm doth lie,
My arm is pretty well wore out and must expire,
Doin' nothin' with that which it was nourished by.
    Well girlie, this makes this season so very long,
    To love this game so well which I must leave ere long.

Humor

Great Correspondence of the Western World:
The Steinbrenner/Machiavelli Letters

꒰

April 3, 1986

Dear Mr. Machiavelli:

Thank you for your recent letter and for your advice about managing a major league baseball team. I particularly like what you have to say that an owner must show himself a lover of ability and merit and that he should honor those who excel upon the field. Honoring the excellent, however, is one thing. Paying exorbitant salaries is another. $2,000,000 a year for anyone who hits above .250 is getting out of hand, don't you think.
In any case, I do appreciate your taking time to write me.

Yours truly,
George Steinbrenner, Owner of the New York Yankees

***

Memo
From GS to Secretary:
Hire Billy Martin.

***

April 17, 1986

Dear Mr. Steinbrenner:

Yours of the 3rd well in hand. I tell you "A man who wishes to make a profession of goodness in everything must necessarily come to grief among so many who are not good. Therefore, it is necessary . . . to learn how not to be good, and to use this knowledge and not use it, according to the necessity of the case."

Yours truly,
Niccolo Machiavelli

***

April 23, 1986

Dear Mr. Machiavelli:

Happy Shakespeare's Birthday (and my critics think I have no culture! Talking to a sportswriter about culture is akin to asking Mother Theresa for birth control information).

Anyway you are right about my being too good for my own good. I think it was Leo "the Lip" Durocher who said "Nice guys finish last." Are you familiar with the history of Baseball? What kind of a season do you have in Florence? Keep it under your hat, but if New York City doesn't cough up some big bucks and an adequate parking lot, there could be a good chance my team could become the Florentine Yanks. If this should come to pass, would you be at all interested in becoming my General Manager? I like your ideas. I think you have a good head on your shoulders.

Yours in haste,
George Steinbrenner

***

Memo (undated)
From GS to secretary:
Fire Billy Martin.

***

May 10, 1986

Dear Mr. Steinbrenner:

Thank you for your offer of the General Managership. It would give me the experience I need to become the owner of my own team. I even have the name all picked out—The New York Nicks. You should keep Billy Martin on.

Yours truly,
Niccolo

***

Memo (undated)
From GS to secretary:
Rehire Billy Martin.

***

May 19, 1986

Dear Niccolo:

I have followed your advice about Billy Martin, but what should I do ·
about Dave Winfield?

Yours,
George

***

May 30, 1986

Dear George:

An owner of a baseball team (hereafter referred to as The Prince) is es-
teemed "when he is a true friend or a true enemy, when, that is, he declares
himself without reserve in favor of some one or against another."

Yours,
Nick

***

June 7, 1986

Dear Nick:

Thanks, I needed that. Too bad you don't work for one of the New York newspapers. Tell me, sir, is it better to be loved or feared?

Yours,
George

***

June 20, 1986

Dear George:

"I conclude, therefore, with regard to being feared and loved, that men love at their own free will, but fear at the will of the prince, and that a wise prince must rely on what is in his power and not on what is in the power of others. . . ."

Yours,
Old Nick

***

July 1, 1986

Dear Nick:

At last, someone who understands me! I have decided to fire Billy Martin and to hire you as manager. Please report to Yankee Stadium by Tuesday afternoon after the All-Star Break. Why aren't we winning the pennant?

Sincerely,
George

***

July 9, 1986

Sorry I could not get released from my contract on such short notice, but I hope I can take over the team in the middle of the 1988 season. I trust Billy Martin could take over for part of that season?

The reason you are losing the pennant is because you have been too kind to your over-paid, overly-pampered players. Need I remind you what the owner of the Romagna Giants did to a surly player named Remirro de Orco? After a few particularly bad games, the owner took the player into the public square at Cesena and in full view of the season ticket holders, de Orca was cut in half. Needless to say, such a display caused the other players on the roster to sit up and take notice.

Yours,
Old Nick

***

Memo From GS to secretary:

Ask Dave Winfeld and Ricky Henderson to meet me at Times Square on the morning of September 1st.

Here the correspondence breaks off. All we have been able to locate are a few more memos regarding the hiring and job placement of Billy Martin. Still, the chance of Niccolo Machiavelli taking over the reins of the New York Yankees this coming season should fill seasoned baseball fans and classical scholars with gleeful anticipation.

The First New York City Baseball Fan
To Be Traded

Ɓ

Many baseball rules are not known by the general public. Rule V, 14, B of the Official Baseball Rule book, for example, has rarely been enforced and came only to my attention in mid-September of this year, when I had the fortune (good or bad? Only the gods can say) of attending a game at Yankee Stadium when the venerable pin-stripes took on the hapless Baltimore Orioles.

A friend of mine had purchased the tickets from an ex-student of his, and very good tickets they were too. We were to be seated in the front row, right behind the catcher. At least I believe they were good tickets. I never got to use mine. As I entered the Stadium, a burly man in a bright red blazer caught my right elbow and quickly led me off to one side. He informed me that I could not take my seat.

"Why?" I asked. I gazed uneasily toward my friend. Had he set me up for some practical joke? Had I been stopped because my loyalties to the Boston Red Sox were widely known? My friend did not look back. He merely hurried on to his choice location in the Stadium. No doubt he believed that whatever minor confusion there was would be quickly cleared and that I would soon join him. Unfortunately, he believed wrong.

The man in the red blazer was quickly joined by five other Security-minded individuals. "You've been traded to San Franscisco," he finally said, though he refused to look me in the eye. He was a big man, some 350 pounds, but his voice was very soft. I had difficulty making out all the words, but the general idea came through.

"Traded? What are you talking about? Has everybody out here gone mad? I'm not even a member of the team!" I mustered as much indignation as I could.

The man reached into his hip pocket and brought forth the rule-book. "You don't understand, sir," he said. "George Steinbrenner has retained the right to trade at least one fan per game." The man in the red blazer read Rule V, 14, B to me: "Any fan who purchases a ticket for a New York Yankees baseball game becomes, from the time he or she enters the ballpark until he or she exits, the exclusive property of the New York Yankees. Such a fan can be activated to the roster, can be traded, or, if necessary, be named interim manager."

I could feel myself go weak in the knees, I have been a baseball fan almost all my life, but I have never read the rule-book from cover to cover.

"But no one has ever enforced this rule before," I sputtered.

The man in the red blazer nodded. "Not until today. Now if you will be so good as to follow me." The guard led me out of the Stadium and toward a black limousine. I certainly had no desire to upset the authorities of the game. Baseball is more important than any one individual, and so I decided to abide by the decision of the baseball commissioner. Seeing that I was not going to fight, the man decided that I was entitled to a bit of more information. "This has been a difficult season," he said, "and Mr. Steinbrenner is in no mood to be trifled with. He has been frustrated all year, and some fans are turning rowdy. He feels that a better class of fan is to be found on the West Coast, and so, for the good of baseball, this trade has been deemed necessary. The limo here will take you straight to La Guardia. Here are first-class plane tickets to San Francisco, and a season pass to the remainder of the Giants' home games. You are expected to be on hand for tomorrow night's game with the Dodgers. Blessings on you. And Good Luck." With those words he placed a Giants' cap upon my head and pushed me into the back seat of the limo.

As the limo pulled away from the Stadium, I turned to see a well-dressed young lady carrying a briefcase. The man in the red blazer carefully placed my ticket into her hand and escorted the woman inside. At least I had some notion for whom I had been traded.

And that is why I have not been home lately. I hope my wife reads this account and realizes that I did not run off with my secretary. I have, of course, been very busy trying to find decent housing and a new job, but I believe I have adjusted to my new team very well. I hope that the trade has worked out well for all concerned. In the meantime, God knows I am doing my best to make Mr. Steinbrenner proud of me.

Aristotle's "On Baseball"
Translated by Louis Phillips

> *"Baseball is Greek, in being national, heroic,*
> *and broken up in the rivalries of city-states."*

ʁ

****

ON BASEBALL

Our subject is the art of baseball in general and the theories of hitting, catching, and pitching in particular, the specific effect of each genre, and the way to play the game so that the sport be pleasing to the eye and soul of the spectator. Let us start, as is proper, with basic principles.

Baseball as Imitation

Dithyrambic baseball, as it was originally named, is the imitation of something, perhaps Tragedy. Perhaps not. In such matters it is difficult to be definitive.

As I have written elsewhere, Comedy is the imitation of inferior men who are not altogether vicious. Thus, the owners of teams are Comedic; the players, with their dreams of immortality and another season in the sun, Tragic.

Derivation of the Word

The term *Baseball* comes from two obscured roots—*baseios*, meaning low, and *ballein*, referring to a type of whale. Hence, the low song of a whale. Or the song of a low whale. How this derivation came about has yet to be determined. Homer maintains that in the early years of the games, when the games were dedicated to the god Poseidon, a whale was sacrificed at the conclusion of each home stand. Unfortunately, the above may well be a folk etymology. After all, everybody knows that Homer frequently preferred a colorful story to the truth.

What scholars do agree upon, especially Danaus and Chaeremon (in spite of his mixed meters), is that baseball was originally called *Baseode*, or Amusement (song) for the low-born.

Whatever the origin of the term, we do know the word was born hundreds of years before *Tragos ode* or Tragedy.

Definition of the Term

Baseball is the good action which is complete and of a certain length (usually nine innings) by means of players who are made pleasing for each of their respective positions; it relies in its various elements not on acting, nor on narrative, but upon skill exhibited within a natural setting; through Pity and Fear, the completed game achieves the cleansing of these emotions. It involves the fall of a team from one level (either of play or of positions in the standings) to a lower level.

The Earliest Use of the Term

The earliest mention of baseball is, of course, to be found in Book VI of Homer's **Odyssey**, where the Princess Nausica tosses a ball. The following passage is of great interest to all scholars of the game and needs, of course, since we are Greek, no translation: "And presently, when Nausica and her maiden servants had finished their lunch, they removed the scarves from their heads and other head-dresses and began playing with a ball. Nausica of the white led them in song."

This passage is of especial interest because it shows that at its inception women were not banned from the game (or *agon*) as they are now.

The Six Elements or Aspects of Dithyrambic Baseball

Every baseball game contains six necessary elements (or seven, if your team is managed by a barbarian) that make the game what it is: Agents, Contracts, Character, Diction, Spectacle, and Music. Most exhibitions of the game involve these elements in much the same manner.

Prophecy and Individual Games

Dithyrambic baseball might well have become more popular in Greece in particular and in Europe, but there is no longer any doubt that its popularity has been dampened by the omnipresence of Tiresias and other prophets addicted to bird prophecy. How disturbing it is to the common mind to have a baseball contest interrupted by the sight of an Eagle flying over the stadiums of Athens and dropping a snake into the lap of the judges. It is even more disturbing to see a prophet tear open a pig or a chicken and spill its entrails across the bleachers—all in the hope of looking for a sign.

Indeed, as Agathon has observed in his monumental **Encyclopedia of**

Dithyrambic Baseball, numerous contests have no sooner gotten underway when Tiresias, blind umpire that he was, would announce the final score. Disgruntled fans would then get up and leave, abandoning the hometown IX for some Dionysian revelry. Who dare blame them? The essence of baseball is the same as the essence of rhetoric—suspense. When suspense is removed from a baseball *agon*, because of vain bubbling of prophets, the game loses all its savor. Indeed, what spectator among us desires to know ahead of time whether or not Oedipus shall hit for the cycle?

It has also been well documented that the Athens Metropolitans lost something in the neighborhood of 580,000 drachmas each and every year they played. No wonder ship owners of certain families near Tampa looked elsewhere to make their fortune.

Until blind prophets are banned from attending the baseball *agon*, the game will certainly suffer a lack of dramatic tension.

The Three Essential Parts

Dithyrambic baseball, as a whole, consists of three parts: the Pitch, the Catch, and the Hit. (I know I have written earlier about the six elements or aspects of the game, but elements are not parts, or if they are parts they are very subtle ones.)

We shall consider each one in turn.

The Pitch is sometimes physical, ofttimes purely linguistic. For example, Androtion, formerly of the A's and now a noted politician, would, after each *agon* or contest, post himself at one of the major exits to the stadium and sell tip sheets to the various chariot races going on about town. He also hawked razors. A number of commentators deplored the pitcher's actions and predicted (correctly) that such pitching would bring forth the mercenary side of players.

The Catch. An old saying goes: like the Pitch, the Catch. What it means is difficult to explain. Allow us to begin with the notion that the Catch possesses a two-fold nature. There is the physical Catch, defined as the act of a fielder (in or out) plucking a battered ball from thin air. And then there is the other kind of Catch, the legal kind which players refer to when perusing the fine print in their contracts. For example, if a player (such as the aforementioned and deplored Androtion) is induced for a substantial bonus to sign a contract with the Spartans so that the Spartans can trade him to Crete for players (or Agonists) to be named later, then the player and/or his agent may rightfully refer to the above play as a Catch.

The Hit. After each game, players have been seen approaching young ladies in the stands and "Hitting" on them. Sometimes, while trying to convince a female fan to join him in a night of debauchery, the player strikes out. Sometimes he gets to first base. This is what players mean most of the time when they talk about Hitting (see Scoring).

Three Additional Elements

Three additional elements of a game may be considered without undue comment. The are Peripety, Discovery, and Suffering. These parts belong properly to the spectators. Especially suffering.

Three Kinds of Games to Be Avoided

There are some forms of the *agon* that should be avoided at all cost:

1. A good team must not be seen passing from happiness to misery because of the misguided actions of its owner.
2. A bad player must not be seen passing from misery to happiness because of a bad bounce or pure chance. Players must act consistent with their skills.
3. An extremely bad *agon* should not be prolonged more than necessary.

Of Baseball and Thought

Thought, most rightly, should be considered in my treatise on Rhetoric, but since Thought occupies a central position in the meaning of the game, we shall mention it here.

Baseball is considered to be boring by the non-thinking. But those who think find the game exciting. This is what is frequently referred to as Athena's Paradox. Athena's Paradox also applies to the rites of Aphrodite.

Indeed, we should also point out that, although everyone on a baseball team thinks, not all members think at the same time. That is why errors occur and why managers have been deemed, by Zeus, as necessary.

As I have said, all members of a baseball team, at some time during a season, think, but for some reason, only the catcher is allowed to adorn himself with the tools of ignorance. This is also a paradox, for the catcher is frequently the most learned player on the field. Some have even been known to take part in the Lenaea in the month of Gamelion. But the comic playwrights deserve what they get.

Antisthenes, the philosopher and protégé of Socrates, insists that excessive squatting (as performed by the catcher) causes the nerves and brains to settle low in the body. Antisthenes is, alas, a cynic.

Baseball and Ritual Murder

Anyone who has set foot inside the bleacher section of a well-contested *agon* has no doubt heard the cry go up:

Kakist' apoloith' ho brabeus

Most evilly may perish the Umpire. This well-known imprecation has sent chills, up and down the spins of novices to the game.

Were umpires actually slaughtered? Yes. After whales were abandoned, umpires were brought in to provide atonement and ritual cleansing. Fortunately, however, because of unionization of the craft of well-seeing and considered judgment, that practice has been rendered unlawful, except in some foreign countries.

But the cry goes on, thus showing us how slowly the rhetoric of the game changes and how eternal baseball truly is.

Yes, Virginia, There Is a Baseball (Perhaps)

Dear Editor:

I am eight years old. Some of my little friends say there is no such thing as baseball. Papa says, "If you see it in *The New Yorker* it's so." Please tell me the truth, Is there such thing as baseball?
Virginia O'Hanlon

Virginia, your little friends are wrong. They have been affected by the publicity of an overhyped age. They do not believe except what they see. They, like so many talk show hosts, think that nothing can be which is not comprehensive to their little minds. All minds, Virginia, whether they belong to television executives or magazine editors, are little. In this expanding universe of ours, human beings are mere insects. A majority leader of the Republican party, in his/her intellect, as compared with the boundless politically correct world about him/her, as measured by recent polls, is not capable of grasping the whole truth and/or knowledge.

Yes, Virginia, there is such thing as baseball. It exists as certainly as prenuptial agreements exist, as certainly as long strikes and MTV. You know that owners of baseball teams abound to give to your life its highest beauty and joy. Alas! How dreary would the world be if there were no baseball. It would be as dreary as if there were no fast food chains. There would be no childhood faith then, no thick tomes of statistics, no baseball encyclopedias, no off-season trades to make tolerable this existence. We should have no enjoyment, except in virtual reality and computer games. The floodlights that illuminate night games would be extinguished.

Not believe in baseball! You might as well not believe in salary caps. You might get your papa/mama to hire men/women to watch all the sports programs on every television channel to catch a glimpse of a baseball game, but even if one were never played, what would that prove? Nobody can afford to go to baseball games anymore, but that is no sign that there is no such thing as baseball. The most real sports in this world are those that men, women, or children, for reasons too numerous to list, can no longer see. Did you ever see a place that paid its school teachers more than it paid baseball players? Of course not, but that's no proof that such places couldn't exist if they wanted to. Outside of *The Field of Dreams*, starring Bud Selig, no one can conceive or imagine all the wonders there are unseen and unseeable in the world.

You can dismantle Yankee Stadium and move it to New Jersey, but there is a veil covering the true spirit of baseball which not the strongest union, nor even the united strength of all the richest owners, can tear apart. Only faith and suborn patience can push aside that veil and view the supernatural beauty beyond. Ah, Virginia, in this world there is nothing else real and abiding.

No baseball! Thank God! Baseball lives and lives forever. A thousand years from now, Virginia, nay 10 times 10,000 years from now, the memory of baseball on real grass will continue to make glad the heart of childhood.

On the other hand....

Roger Clemens, Orel Hershiser,
Frank Viola, and Me

I do not think Roger Clemens, Orel Hershiser, Frank Viola, and myself could ever form the three-and-a-half musketeers. It's not that I don't respect the abilities of these major league pitchers. It's just that I am too envious of them. I also feel I am deserving of an $8 million, three-year, iron-clad contract for my singular abilities on the pitching mound, even if my skills differ significantly in scope and intent from theirs.

For one thing, Clemens, Hershiser, and Viola pitch to the best hitters major league owners can buy, whereas my pitching is limited to tossing tennis balls to my three-year-old sons and their friends. It is one thing to toss a baseball so that a batter swings at it and misses—that, no doubt, is a valuable skill. Yet, regardless of what any hotshot agent says, it is far more difficult to toss a ball so that a three-year-old child can hit it, and hit it with authority.

When Viola pitches, his sole thought is: How can I get this (expletives deleted) batter out. When I pitch, my thoughts are different. I must consider the feelings and limitations of the batter. If the batter should swing and miss too often, he or she may well become discouraged and give up on the sport entirely.

How do I pitch the ball in such a way that a three-year-old can slug it? To answer that question, I must take into account the distance from batter to pitcher, the composition of the bat (plastic, wood, aluminum, or other), the velocity and direction of the wind, how much the batter weighs, how tall the batter is, the tendency of the batter to swing high or low, the eye preference of the batter, the size and weight of the ball (tennis ball, rubber spaldeen, plastic whiffle ball, or other), the contour of the batter's box (if there is one), and the general mood of the child. Then, calling on over 40 years of superb and tireless training, I must throw the ball with such precise timing and placement that it will hit the bat, thus giving the child the illusion that he or she is indeed Babe Ruth or Lou Gehrig.

Go on, Roger and Orel and Frankie—I defy you to do as much. Anybody can throw a hard curve at the corner of the plate, where no civilized person would dare to swing! That's nothing compared with what other playground pitchers and I do day in and day out. And most of us don't have months of spring training in Florida, either.

One more thing, you guys—when you strike out an opposing batter and reduce his wife and loved ones to tears, you have no need to consider the feelings of your victim. Whereas I, upon taking the concrete mound of some makeshift playground (with no grounds keeper to manicure the fields into picture-postcard shape), have to be part Joe DiMaggio and part Mother Theresa.

No satisfaction for me when I lay in a perfect strike. Oh, no! Should the three-year-old batter swing at my palm ball and miss, I cannot turn away with a malicious and self-serving grin. No way. I must immediately begin shouting words of encouragement. "Almost . . . You nearly hit that one . . . Good swing . . . You're going to get a homer on the next one. Here it comes . . . Just keep your eye on the ball."

I would love to see the day in Fenway Park when Nolan Ryan, the man with the $3 million arm, stands on the mound, shouting to Wade Boggs: "Here it comes, Wade. A fast ball down the middle. Keep your eye on it. Just swing level and try to get wood on it." It will never happen in my lifetime.

And so, Roger, Orel, and Frankie—I don't care how many millions you wheel home in your barrows. As far as I'm concerned, you guys are just pikers. Amateurs. Putzers. When you can throw a baseball in such a way that a three- or four-year-old can hit it, when you can pitch with such precision that a toddler feels like the next Ted Williams or Jim Rice or Don Mattingly, then you can talk to me. You can hang around my locker. You can carry my glove. Until then, boys, take your contracts and stuff 'em. I got it all over you, and don't think I don't know it.

Bard at Bat
Shakespeare Makes Baseball's Greatest Plays

ⱕ

AT ONE TIME, SHAKESPEARE OWNED PART INTEREST IN A BALL CLUB—the Stratford Variorums—and this team once played a series of exhibition games against a team consisting of America's all-time great players. The night of the season opener, Shakespeare and his sister invited me to attend the game with them. We were unfortunately late in arriving at the ball park, so Shakespeare hurried me to my seat:

SHAKESPEARE: "But sirrah, make haste, Percy is already in the field." *(I Henry IV, IV, ii, 74-75)*

It took me a moment to realize that Shakespeare was referring to his centerfielder—Joe Percy. Falstaff, the manager of the Variorums, came onto the field to change pitchers. Falstaff wanted a fresh hurler to face Ruth.

ME: Tell me, who's your catcher?

SHAKESPEARE: "Passion, I see, is catching." *(Caesar III, i 283)*

ME: Number 38, Yogi Passion, catcher. This is a strange line-up.

SHAKESPEARE: "Now name the rest of the players." *(A Midsummer Night's Dream, I, ii 39)*

ME: We have Hector Richmond in right field, Joe Percy in center, Jory Richmond in left, Al Richmond at third, Ajax Richmond at second, Laertes Richmond at first, Titus Richmond at short. . . .

SHAKESPEARE: "I think there be six Richmonds in the field." *(Richard III, V, iv, 11)*

Claudius let fly with a fast ball. Ruth hit a towering fly to right.

SHAKESPEARE: "Hector shall have a great catch." *(Troilus and Cressida, II, i, 99-100)*

HECTOR *(to himself, in right field)*: "I'll catch it ere it come to ground."

(*Macbeth, III, v 25*)

Alas, Hector did not catch it. He overran the ball, scoring Mantle from second.

SHAKESPEARE: "Here Aaron is; and what with Aaron now?" (*Titus Andronicus, IV, ii 54*)

ME: A home run, I should guess.

SHAKESPEARE: "Strike him, Aumerle." (*Richard II, V, ii 85*)

Hank pounded a hard grounder to the first baseman, Ruth broke for third.

SHAKESPEARE: "Come, for the third, Laertes, you do but dally." (*Hamlet, V, ii, 297*)

Laertes fired a perfect strike to the third baseman, Ruth hit the dirt.

SHAKESPEARE: "The foot slides. . . ." (*Troilus and Cressida, III, iii, 215*)

ME: That was a great throw from Laertes!

Ruth leapt to his feet and began to argue the call. Billy Martin, manager of the All-Stars stormed out of the dugout.

SHAKESPEARE'S SISTER: Be calm, brother. Let the umpire decide the question.

SHAKESPEARE: "There is three umpires in the matter I understand." (*The Merry Wives of Windsor, I, i 137*)

ME: The Babe was safe!

SHAKESPEARE: "Out, dog, out, cur!" (*A Midsummer Night's Dream, III, ii 65*)

ME: Safe! Al missed the tag!

SHAKESPEARE: "Out, I say!" (*Macbeth, I, i 35*)

Martin was finally ejected from the game. Al Simmons stepped to the plate.

ME: He's going to hit it.

SHAKESPEARE (*taunting the batter*): "Thou canst not hit it, hit it, hit it. Thou canst not hit it, my good man." (*Love's Labor's Lost, IV, i, 125-126*)

The pitch was thrown. Simmons swung, missed, and missed again. Edwin Snider was announced as the next batter. He hit a pop fly to Percy.

ME: It's an easy out. . . . Percy's under it.

SHAKESPEARE: "No doubt but he hath got a quiet catch." *(Taming of the Shrew, II, i, 331)*

The lead of the American All-Stars held up. Nonetheless, Shakespeare had completely fallen under the spell of baseball. As he and I and his sister left the stadium he turned to me and said:

"I'll make a journey twice as far t'enjoy a second night of such sweet shortness." *(Cymbeline, II, iv 43-44)*

If the Signers of the Declaration of Independence Acted the Way Modern Baseball Players Do

Dear Tom:

Your declaration of independence from Britain looks fine to me. I would, of course, be happy to sign it, but you realize of course that I had a good season last year. Therefore, I must charge the Continental Congress fifty dollars for my signature.

Sincerely,

John Adams
(letter-pressed, but not signed)

***

Dear Mr. Jefferson:

Thank you for your kind invitation to sign the Declaration. I hope you realize that I charge a minimum of $35 per autograph. If the Continental Congress will send me a cashiers check by messenger, I shall be in Philadelphia by July 4th.

Yours,

Button Gwinnett
(letter dictated, but not signed)

***

Dear Thomas:

Your Declaration of Independence from the mad king is some piece of writing. I would be happy to sign it, but, alas, I must charge you $25* per autograph. You know how it is these days. I have a lot of mouths to feed.

Samuel Chase
(not signed in his absence)

* Cash only. No checks!

***

Yo Tom!

Okay. I'll sign it. But I must have $30 per autograph. I don't sign uniforms either. Have the Continental Congress leave the cash in a plain brown satchel at my hotel.

Yours on the way to Phillie,

John Witherspoon
(printed, not signed)

Information on the Back of
the Old Baseball Card:

Thomas Muldoone, Jr.
Pitcher. Boston Red Stockings

Although Tom "The Buzzard" Muldoone
appeared in only 15 games last season,
he was the only A.L. pitcher to post a
perfect won-lost average!

MAJOR AND MINOR LEAGUE PITCHING RECORD

	Games	innings	won	lost	Pct.	SO	Walks	E.R.A.
YEAR	15	30	4	0	1.000	15	12	3.00

Information on the Back of
the New Baseball Card:

Thomas J. Muldoone, III, ESQ.

Pitcher. Cincinnati Reds
Depositor: CitiBank

Mr. Muldoone appeared in only 15 games last season, but he was paid more than $700,000 for each appearance, setting a new club record. Indeed, 1995 was Mr. Muldoone's finest season for world-wide investments, with his portfolio amassing a 19% increase, a new N.L. record. Mr. Muldoone's stocks opened slowly with Union Carbide and Rockwell Institute Trust, but he was able to bounce back later in the season by switching to real estate and tax-free municipal bonds. He holds 13 major-league investment records.

Cosi Fans Tutti:
The Granddaddy of Baseball Operas To Make Its Presence Felt

Although there are literally tens of popular songs about baseball, there are (alas!) very few operas about the sport. Thus, the recent discovery of an unproduced opera by Stengel and Hayden has caused a great stir in music circles. (It actually doesn't take very much to cause a great stir in music circles, for such circles stir quite easily; any scrap of manuscript paper is likely to cause a fuss.) The opera, entitled **Cosi Fans Tutti**, was nearly completed, at the untimely death of Stengel and the most untimely death of Hayden, and was discovered under a pile of unpaid bills.

As of this writing, the Metropolitan Opera is planning a production in the Spring of 2001.

Cosi Fans Tutti: Opera Comique/Tragique

Scene: San Francisco/Oakland/Vienna/Athens/other unreal cities

Time: December, 198—,199—

Chief Characters:　　*The Queen of Portugal*
　　　　　　　　　　The Count of the Baseball Commission
　　　　　　　　　　Colonel Fairfax
　　　　　　　　　　Fax
　　　　　　　　　　Club Owners
　　　　　　　　　　Mark of Langston
　　　　　　　　　　Mark of Davis
　　　　　　　　　　Kirby of Puckett
　　　　　　　　　　Count di Box Office Receipts
　　　　　　　　　　Parsifal
　　　　　　　　　　Kundy
　　　　　　　　　　Satyagraha
　　　　　　　　　　and numerous fans

The story of Cosi Fans Tutti is taken from a medieval legend (circulated by owners of major league teams, who have reluctantly abandoned stories of poisoned wells). The time is late in the 1980s or some era in the dark ages. The Burgomeister and Commissioner of Baseball stand at the window of a high-rise owned by G. Steinbrenner.

"'Habit is a great Deadener,' said Samuel Beckett," the Commissioner sings. "But so too is playing for a losing team," the Burgomeister replies.

Outside the high-rise in a peaceful part of the Bronx on the bank of the East River, a tribe of Gypsy free agents have pitched their tents and temporary condominiums. A bright fire is burning, and a hungry band of pitchers, catchers, outfielders, infielders, and designated hitters have gathered to pray to their agents. They fall to their knees and sing the beautiful and touching religious hymn, "More."

> More! More! More! More!
> More! More! More! More!
> *Si li Conosco!* [1]

The touching but beautiful hymn is interrupted by the arrival of a first baseman named Don M. Alfonso. Alfonso is greeted with much warmth as he sings, *"Tutti, lor piante, tutti deliri loro ancor tu sai,"* which, freely translated, means, "then you have noticed the owners of major league clubs are overcome by desperation?"

More contracts are tossed on the fire and there is much dancing and singing (simple peasant songs mingled with Gregorian Chants). These baseball players and agents are simple, happy wanderers following their hearts from place to place.

The leader of the players, a venerable young lawyer, whose eyes are young but sad—steps forward, dances a minuet with the Burgomeister (who has donned a disguise to spy on the players) and sings what is known in musicology as "The Lawyer's Aria"[2]

> *Ah, perdon mio bel diletto*
> *Innocenyi e questo cor*
>
> (I am sure the owners' opposition
> and their fierce anger is not for show)
>
> (translation by Hrbek)

All eyes now turn toward Langston and his fast ball. Years before, Langston had come as a stranger to the tribe, declaring himself weary of the trials and disappointments of life in an obscure part of the media marketplace. He begged to be allowed to remain for a short time with the Gypsies or Free Agents, who received him with great courtesy and hospitality.

From off-stage (Queens?) we hear the screams of thousands of men, women, and children. Thirty thousand[3] die-hard baseball fans rush onto the stage, singing *"Gusti nuni cosa a sento?"* ("How dare a .237 hitter demand a salary of over three million a year?")

The fans pay ten or fifteen dollars for the privilege of doing a little dance with the players. This dance, a combination of a waltz and a mere bagatelle, lasts most of the winter. At the conclusion, the fans leap high into the air and chant, *"Ah che piu non ho ritegno"* (Now I am thoroughly disgusted").

The penultimate scene of the opera is perhaps the most touching one of all. The teenaged daughter of a third baseman who cannot break the million dollar per season salary structure feels that her family name is shamed beyond redemption. She takes down from the wall a Japanese sword, brought back by her lover, a major league player who had spent two or three years with the Hiroshima Carps. She kisses the blade and tenderly remembers that he had used the sword to commit harry-carey. When Pinkerton returns, searching for a no-trade option and some betting slips bearing the autograph of a future Hall-of-Famer, he sees the body of his mistress. He cries out in despair, and turns to face the ghost of R.D. Laing (whose spirit hovers over the scene). The ghost shrieks, "Long before thermonuclear war can come about we have had to lay waste our sanity."

For the final scene we cut to a secret meeting of the baseball owners who are dressed in hair shirts and who are beating themselves with sacred boughs from Louisville. As the curtain finally descends, all the owners stand and sing a tribute to their players: "I Love Them Like a Father."

The theater fills with *"Sono i piu dolci amici ch'io m'abbia in questio mondo, e vostri ancor saranno!"*

Notes

[1]Some consider this a misprint for Canseco. Consult his toll-free number for clarification

[2]Not to be confused with "The Lawyer's Recitative."

[3]Obviously some doubling and tripling of parts is called for.

Drama

Babe in the Woods

᠍

A WOOD. A STRANGE WOOD. A LAYER OF MIST OR FOG UPON THE GROUND. A SINGLE TREE IN A STATE OF TWISTED NERVOUS COLLAPSE. ON THE TREE SITS OWL. NOT TO MISLEAD ANYONE, OWL IS A MAN IN HIS MID-FORTIES. HE IS OF MODERATE BUILD AND WEARS A DARK BROWN SUIT. HE SITS QUIETLY AMID STRANGE VEGETATION. HE READS *THE WALL STREET JOURNAL.* IN THE BACKGROUND, WE CAN HEAR A LOUDSPEAKER AT YAN-KEE STADIUM MAKING ITS ANNOUNCEMENT: *"And now batting for the New York Yankees, No. 3, George Herman Ruth."* THE ANNOUNCE-MENT, AS YOU MIGHT EXPECT, IS GREETED BY GREAT CHEERS.

AND SO, AS YOU MIGHT *NOT* EXPECT, ENTER BABE RUTH. HE IS IN THE PRIME OF HIS CAREER, WEARING HIS FAMOUS NEW YORK YANKEE PINSTRIPES, AND CARRYING TWO BATS.

BABE RUTH (STOPS. LOOKS AROUND)
Hey. . . . What the . . .

OWL (NOT LOOKING UP FROM HIS PAPER)
Hmmm?

BABE RUTH
What's going on here?

OWL (LOOKING UP)
Sorry.

BABE RUTH (GENUINELY BEWILDERED)
Where's home plate? What in the hell have you done with home plate?. . . Where did everybody go?

OWL
Just what is home plate?

BABE RUTH
What do you mean, what is home plate? I'm stepping out of the dugout, the score is six to three, with the lousy St. Louis Browns ahead. . . . The

BABE RUTH
bases are loaded, I'm going to the plate, ready to win this game in the
bottom of the ninth . . . and what the hell is going on? I end up here.

OWL
There's no need to yell. I don't understand what you're talking about.

BABE RUTH
You don't understand what I'm talking about?

OWL
Not really. . . . No.

BABE RUTH
I'm talking baseball, that's what I'm talking. I'm talking about walking
from the dugout to home plate, and ending up standing here with a bunch
of rhubarb growing at my feet.

OWL
It's poison ivy, actually.

BABE RUTH
Poison Ivy? (LEAPS OUT). I can't get poison ivy. Poison ivy is for pitchers.
It's not for home run hitters. . . . I can't play baseball if I'm covered
with poison ivy. What kind of cheap trick is this?

OWL
I'm sorry. I don't know what baseball is either.

BABE RUTH
You don't know what baseball is? What are you? A commie?

OWL
Commie?

BABE RUTH
Communist. You ain't American, that's for certain.

OWL
I was born in Spokane.

BABE RUTH
Not if you don't know what baseball is.

OWL
Actually I have an excuse . . . I'm an owl.

BABE RUTH
O.K., so you're an owl. That's not an excuse. That's a mental sickness.

OWL
I really am an owl.

BABE RUTH
So what does that make me?

OWL
I don't know. What does it make you?

BABE RUTH
It makes me the Big Toe on the King of England, that's what it makes me.

OWL
Okay. If you want to be the Big Toe on the King of England, suit yourself.

BABE RUTH
I don't want to be the Big Toe on the King of England. I want to be what I am.

OWL
I want to be what I am too. And since we're both what we want to be, why aren't we happier?

BABE RUTH
I am happy . . . I'm Babe Ruth, for chrissakes.

OWL (HOLDS OUT A TALON)
Pleased to meet you. I'm Owl.

BABE RUTH
So you say. . . . Don't owls have names?

OWL
Not if no one names you.

BABE RUTH (THINKING IT OVER)
Oh, I get it. This is another one of Miller Huggins' practical jokes . . . I mean this is one of the most extravagant practical jokes in the history of baseball. I guess everyone's getting tired of hotfeet and dropping grape fruit off the Washington Monument. The good and tried practical jokes don't suit the likes of the New York Yankees. Not only we got to win the pennant, we got to win the World Series of practical jokes.

OWL
What's a practical joke?

BABE RUTH
Come on. Get off it. You're talking to the Babe! The Babe wasn't born yesterday.

OWL
If you weren't born yesterday, then why do they call you *Baby*?

BABE RUTH
They don't call me the Baby. They call me the Babe. Short for Bambino. That's Italian.

OWL
Well, if Bambino is Italian, then what's the big stink about me not being an American?

BABE RUTH
Are you going to pretend you never heard of Babe Ruth? The Great Bambino. The Sultan of Swat. I make more money than the President of the United States.

OWL
So do I.

BABE RUTH
Smart guy. I thought you said you were an owl.

OWL
I am an owl. But I'm an investing owl. Why do you think owls are so smart? We're not like other birds. We live off our investments. Live off the interest, and never touch the principal. I can't think of a better motto than that.

BABE RUTH
I can. Try, "Stick this bat up your ass!"

OWL
Somehow I don't think of that as a motto.

BABE RUTH
Well, sit tight. Someday it will become the motto of the United States. You want a piece of advice?

OWL
Only if it's as good as "Live off the interest and never touch the principal." . . . Actually, I have never heard a piece of advice any better than that. So you might as well save your breath.

BABE RUTH
Don't make fools out of people. You won't live long that way.

OWL
I wasn't making a fool out of you. I was just sitting here, minding my own business, wondering if I should get into a tax-free municipal bond fund or not.

BABE RUTH
I'm going back where I came from.

OWL
All the way back to the womb?

BABE RUTH
Not that far back. Just to Yankee Stadium. . . . Which way did I come?

OWL
I didn't notice.

BABE RUTH
No. Of course not. When I get my hands on Huggins, he's dead meat. Nobody plays this kind of a joke on me.

    THE BABE DISAPPEARS INTO THE FOREST. AFTER A FEW SEC-
ONDS OF RUMMAGING AROUND HE RETURNS.

OWL
Back already?

BABE RUTH
Don't get funny with me! . . . (POINTS TOWARD A NEW DIRECTION)
I'm going out that way.

OWL
I wouldn't if I were you.

BABE RUTH
Why not?

OWL
Because of the quicksand. That way is all full of quicksand.

BABE RUTH
Right. And I'm the Pope's behind.

OWL
Anything's possible.

RUTH GOES OFF. WE LISTEN. WE HEAR A PLOP. A CRY. THEN
HIM SHOUTING: "HELP, HELP. I'M DROWNING IN QUICKSAND!"
OWL GOES ON READING HIS NEWSPAPER. FINALLY THE UNDER-
GROWTH PARTS AND TWO STRONG WOMEN (LAURA and JOBSON)
DRESSED IN LONG, GREEN VICTORIAN DRESSES ENTER CARRY-
ING (OR, IF NECESSARY DRAGGING ON A LITTER) THE GREAT
BAMBINO. THE BABE IS COVERED WITH VINES AND LEAVES. HIS
CAP IS TURNED AROUND, BUT HE STILL CARRIES HIS BATS.

LAURA
Look at what we found!

JOBSON
He was exploring the quicksand.

BABE RUTH
I wasn't exploring it. I was drowning in it.

LAURA
Well, drowning is one way of exploring!

OWL
It's just not the most efficient. Besides, I'm not certain it's correct to call it drowning. It's closer to suffocation. You open your mouth and sand pours in, then it clogs up your nostrils. The secret to surviving quicksand, like the secret to surviving anything in life, is to relax, give yourself up to it. And to let go of the bats.

BABE RUTH
Putting quicksand into the batter's box! How low can practical jokes go? What's wrong with just putting shaving cream on top of someone's cap? Isn't that good enough for them?

LAURA
I couldn't believe it. He wouldn't let go of those bats for anything.

BABE RUTH
There's a game in progress, see? I'm up. I'm on the way to the plate, the bases are loaded, the score's six to three in favor of the Browns, and everybody's waiting for me to hit a home run. What am I supposed to hit a home run with? My Big Toe?

OWL
How long have you had this Big Toe fixation?

JOBSON
What's a home run?

LAURA
Who are the Browns? Are you certain you don't mean brownies?

BABE RUTH
Don't tell me you haven't heard of baseball either.

LAURA
No. But that's no reason to be angry with us.

JOBSON
After all, we did save your life. That should count for something.

LAURA
No one takes saving life as seriously as they once did.

BABE RUTH
I am Babe Ruth, all-American hero. Every boy standing in the sandlot
between here and Spokane wants to be me!

LAURA
Shy, isn't he?

JOBSON
Modesty used to be a virtue. Now it's whoever can cry, "I'm the greatest!"

LAURA
And why are you being so sexist? What do little girls want to be?

BABE RUTH
They don't want to be me. That's for certain.

JOBSON
Or don't little girls get the opportunity to stand in the middle of sandlots,
dreaming of whatever you call it. Baseball.

BABE RUTH
Look, Owl, help me! I should be in Yankee Stadium, but I'm drowning
in quicksand!

JOBSON
If you didn't wish to drown in quicksand, you shouldn't have gotten into
it in the first place.

LAURA
After all, there is not much else a person can do in quicksand but drown
in it. You can't build a house on it.

BABE RUTH
Did Higgins bribe everyone on the universe to gang up on me?

JOBSON
What do people do in baseball anyway?

BABE RUTH
Someone pitches the ball, someone hits the ball, then the person who hits
the ball runs around the bases, from first to second to third to home, and
scores a run. The team that scores the most runs wins.

OWL
Sounds very intelligent.

BABE RUTH
All right. So it's not brain surgery. But it keeps a lot of people happy. It gives them something to think about when they're tired of thinking.

OWL
Owls never get tired of thinking.

LAURA
Nor do nymphomaniacs. . . . At least, that's what I've heard. (TO HER SISTER) Don't look at me like that.

OWL
I think what you should do is turn in your bats for an axe.

BABE RUTH
What do I want an axe for?

OWL
To chop down trees, build shelter. A baseball bat is not going to do you much good out here.

BABE RUTH
I'm not going to play Paul Bunyan! I want to go home!

LAURA
I feel home is overrated, don't you?

BABE RUTH
Not me. I was an orphan. I have a hankering for home. . . . Look, I've got batters on base. They've announced my name. If I don't get up to the plate, thousands of fans are going to be disappointed. I'm going to get such a fine it'll take me a year to pay if off.

BABE RUTH GOES OFF INTO THE UNDERGROWTH

JOBSON
Stubborn, isn't he?

OWL
I think it's feathers that gives the mind flexibility. The ability to soar.

LAURA
And not wearing shoes. Once you're cut off from Mother Earth, the brain goes stale.

JOBSON
Poor human beings.

LAURA
It's hard to think anything good to say about them.

BABE RUTH RETURNS. HE IS COVERED WITH BRIARS.

BABE RUTH
All right. Where is it? What have you done to Yankee Stadium?

OWL
We haven't done a thing to it.

BABE RUTH
Am I trapped here forever?

OWL
I don't know, but why don't you try to make the best of it?

BABE RUTH
I'm a baseball player, not the Jolly Woodsman.

LAURA
What's so great about being a baseball player?

BABE RUTH
I didn't say it was great. But it's who I am. It's great for me. I just want to get up to the plate. And hit the ball. It's all I want to do. It was what I was meant to do. When I swing, everybody stops to watch. Everybody. The President. The King. The Pope. God Himself might lean out of Heaven and think that is what my Kingdom is about, that there is nothing more beautiful than a person . . . or even a loony animal—plants even . . .doing what they are meant to do. And that's what I'm doing . . . I'm on my way to do it. Why don't you practical jokers get out of my way?

OWL
We're not in your way.

BABE RUTH
Well, something's in my way. Everytime I go out, I end up back here.

LAURA
It's not the worst place in the world to be.

BABE RUTH
For me it is. There is nothing here that remotely smells of hot dogs and beer. . . . God, I hate it out here. Nothing to do. There's green stuff out here that shouldn't be seen in shower stalls.

OWL
It's just not what you're used to.

BABE RUTH
I don't want to get used to it. A man's meant to do something, you know.

OWL
And owls aren't, I guess.

BABE RUTH
I wasn't talking about you. I was talking about me.

OWL
Maybe if you talked about somebody else for a change, you would be happier.

BABE RUTH
I don't care about happiness. Happiness is for wimps. I want to hit home runs. When I come up to bat, I want the moon to back up.

JOBSON
What happens when you can't play whatever you call it anymore?

BABE RUTH
Baseball!

JOBSON
I guess you can't do it forever. Right?

OWL
Stands to reason.

BABE RUTH
I'll come to that bridge when I cross it. I ain't there yet.

OWL
Maybe you are.

BABE RUTH
All right. Maybe I am. Maybe the Great Scorer who chalks against our
names has tacked up George Herman Ruth and is busy chalking away,
but what am I supposed to do about it? Fall down and cry and beg for mercy?

LAURA
Change.

BABE RUTH
Let the whole world change . . . not me! You want me to be your woods
man? I'll be your woodsman. I'll show you. I'll take Black Betsy and
whack the hell out of some poor tree until Nature cries for mercy.

HE DOES SO. BECOMING ALARMINGLY VIOLENT.

OWL
Stop it! Someone is going to get hurt.

BABE RUTH (STOPS HITTING THE INNOCENT TREE)
So what? I'm being hurt too! By not being allowed to get up to bat! . . . I
know to wise birds like you, that what I ask out of life is laughable, that
in the Great Scheme of Things, which cannot be completely seen from
right field or from the batter's box, that in the meaningful expansion of
the universe that the hitting of a ninety-mile-per-hour fast ball from the
hand of a pitcher that wants to fake you out of your jock, is not the most
serious act a human being can perform, except for one small fact that
must be considered—there is beauty to it. It is honest. And it doesn't
harm anyone too much. . . . Besides, it's all I can do.

JOBSON
He makes baseball sound like sex.

BABE RUTH
Sometimes baseball is better than anything. It is the most beautiful creation ever devised by human beings on this planet. Poetry cannot hold a candle to it. Nor mathematics.

OWL
Or swooping down and ripping the guts out of a field mouse.

LAURA
That sounds like sex too. . . .

WE HEAR THE LOUDSPEAKER AT YANKEE STADIUM ANNOUNCING BABE RUTH'S NAME. THE CHEER OF THE CROWD.

BABE RUTH
They're calling for me. I have to go.

OWL
You don't give up easily, do you?

BABE RUTH
That's what pitchers want me to do, but if I did, how could I have ever hit sixty home runs?

BABE RUTH EXITS.

LAURA (CALLING AFTER HIM)
Not everyone gets to play, I bet . . . (BACK TO OWL) I bet a lot of humans never get a chance.

LAURA GOES OUT IN THE GENERAL DIRECTION OF RUTH'S EXIT.

OWL
Maybe we should learn how to play that baseball of his.

JOBSON
Why?

OWL
It might be fun.

JOBSON
I can't think of anything more boring than games. If plants played games, there wouldn't be enough oxygen to breathe.

LAURA RETURNS. SHE HOLDS BABE RUTH'S CAP.

LAURA
I warned him. If he falls into the quicksand again, I think we should just let him go.

JOBSON
Did you think he was cute?

LAURA
Too heavy to be cute . . . His cap is cute.

OWL
Everyday something falls out of the heaven with a heavy thud.

WE HEAR THE SOUND OF A BALL BEING HIT. CHEERS. NEW YORK YANKEE ANNOUNCER: "And there goes the Great Bambino rounding the bases. The Yankees win 7 to 6. The Yankees clinch the pennant. The Yankees clinch the pennant."

OWL
Something so heavy that mortals cannot even pick it up.

LAURA
Well, I hope he's happy now.

JOBSON
Who?

LAURA
Whoever he was, playing his silly game.

OWL (TAKING UP HIS PIPE AND FILLING IT)
I doubt it.

LAURA
Why? It sounds like he hit his home run.

OWL
No. Does he have the swiftness of the deer? The eyesight of the eagle?
The wisdom of owl? Does he have the cunning of the fox? The sheer
grace of the gazelle? No, I know these humans. I know what he's thinking,
rounding the bases, pounding for home. With something chill at his heels,
and the dust rising behind him, I know what's going through that minuscule,
peanut-sized brain of his.

LAURA
You do?

OWL
I do.

JOBSON
Well, wise old owl, tell us. What is he thinking, running those bases?

OWL (LIGHTING HIS PIPE)
Something else. . . . He's thinking of something else.

LIGHTS OUT.

THE END

Louis Phillips' most recent book is *Ask Me Anything About Baseball,* from Avon Books. He has written and published novels, poetry, humor, and non-fiction, including *Theodore Jonathon Wainwright Is Going To Bomb the Pentagon, How Do You Get a Horse Out of the Bath Tub,* and *The Time, The Hour, The Solitariness of the Place.* Mr. Phillips lives in New York City and teaches at The School of Visual Arts.

Recent fiction from Livingston Press:

Alabama Bound, stories by 26 authors, including Albert Murray, Tobias Wolff, Madison Jones, Helen Norris, Mary Ward Brown, Barry Hannah, William Cobb, and Eugene Walter. **James Colquitt, editor. $13.95**

A Bad Piece of Luck, black humor set in Tampa, Florida, this novel's voice is one you won't forget. **Tom Abrams, author. 9.95**

Sideshows, this first collection has an array of dazzling voices and tones. Set in Alabama. **B.K. Smith, author. $10.95**

Forthcoming fiction, all due in early Fall 1996:

Sixteen Reasons Why I Killed Richard M. Nixon, a novel about our reaction to the man nearly everyone loved to hate. **L.A. Heberlein, author.**

Let Go the Glass Voice, about an Irish family, this novel twists in an intriguing psychological maze that belies its brevity. **Maureen McCafferty, author. $ 9.95**

Don Quickshot, a comic novel—in verse, no less—about a modern day Mafia Don on a vengeance trail in South America. Windmills *forboden.* **William Van Wert, author. $ 9.95.**